PLUCKING FROM FIG TREES

Plucking from Fig Trees

KASIAH HARRISON

Eileen Publishers

Contents

Chapter 1

شمس "Sun"

In the lush gardens of the Alcazar, hidden from prying eyes, Aurya and Safwan stole another fleeting moment of their forbidden love. The full moon cast a pale ghetto upon the fountains, their tinkling waters offering a semblance of privacy to the illicit lovers. Aurya's heart pounded in her chest, the sound drowned out only by the crashing waves of the nearby sea. Safwan's strong arms enveloped her, his embrace a balm to her weary soul.

"My Aurya," he whispered, his voice awash with longing, "I cannot bear this any longer. I must tell my mother of our love, of our plans to be wed."

A shiver ran down her spine, and not from the cool night air. "Safwan, no," she pleaded, her dark eyes reflecting the conflicting desires in her heart. "You know she will never approve of me, a Moorish noble's daughter, as your bride."

He brushed a strand of her ebony hair from her face, his fingertips leaving a trail of fire in their wake. "I will not live another day without you as my wife, my queen by my side. I am the heir to the throne, I will not be denied."

Reluctantly, Aurya nodded, her determination steeled by his unwavering devotion. "Very well, my love. I shall inform my family of your intentions."

The next day, Safwan set out to break the news to his mother, hidden apprehension gnawing at his heart. He found her in the lush gardens of their palace, overseeing the planting of rare orchids from a far-off land. The sunlight caught the jewels in her opulent headdress, casting a crown of fire upon her head.

"Mother," he began, dropping to one knee before her, "I have news."

Queen Aisha's eyes narrowed, her gaze as cold and unforgiving as the emeralds in her regal headpiece. "Rise, my son, and speak your mind."

Taking a deep breath, Safwan revealed his intentions to marry Aurya, the daughter of Lord Alcazar. The queen's expression darkened, her once-beautiful features contorting in disgust.

"You cannot mean to wed that... that Moorish wench," she spat, her voice dripping with venom. "Have you lost all sense, Safwan? Your duty is to our people, to our bloodline!"

"But, Mother—"

"Silence!" she thundered, her words cutting him off like a scythe through wheat. "Your choice of bride is not yours to make. I have already selected a suitable match for you: Princess Jamila, daughter of the Spanish royal house. Our alliance will strengthen our position in the eyes of both the Moors and the Christians."

Safwan's heart ached at the thought of betraying Aurya, but he knew he could not defy his mother's will. Bowing his head in submission, he choked out his obedience. As he left the garden, red-eyed and heavy-hearted, the newly-planted orchids withered and died, their once-vibrant petals crumbling to ashes in the scorching sunlight – an omen of the doomed love that would never blossom under his mother's iron rule.

Meanwhile, Aurya paced the halls of her father's palace, her heart in turmoil. She had been summoned to meet with him in the hour of the serpent, a time reserved for matters of great importance or dire news. The midday heat did nothing to quell the chill that settled in her bones as she entered the chujra, the women's quter, where her father waited.

"Father," she said, bowing low before him. "What is this urgent news you wish to share?"

Lord Alcazar's face was etched with lines of worry, his dark eyes boring into hers. "Rise, my daughter. I have received a proposal of marriage for you."

A shiver ran down Aurya's spine. "From whom, Father?"

"The very same house Safwan is to wed into: the Spanish royal family," he said, the words tumbing out like bile. "Prince Rodrigo, Jamila's twin brother, has set his sights on you."

The room spun around Aurya, and for a moment, she feared she might faint. Her vision blurred, the intricate geometric patterns of the floor blending together like the threads of a tapestry stained with blood. Safwan, her Safwan, was to wed another.

Steeling herself, Aurya lifted her chin, determination hardening her features. "I will not accept," she vowed, her voice firm and unwavering. "My heart belongs to Safwan, and only him."

Lord Alcazar's face darkened, and he rose from his cushions to tower over her. "You will do as you are told, Aurya!" he thundered. "The honor of our family, the very survival of our people, depends on this union. You will marry Prince Rodrigo, and you will bear him strong heirs!"

Aurya's heart shattered into a thousand jagged shards, each one a reminder of the impossible situation she found herself in. She knew her father spoke the truth; her duty to her family and her people far outweighed her own desires. With a heavy heart, she bowed her head, submitting to her fate. "As you wish, Father."

In the days that followed, Aurya went through the motions of preparing for her wedding with a leaden heart. Safwan, ever the honorable and duty-bound prince, did not once try to dissuade her from her course, but his eyes betrayed the depth of his anguish. They met in secret as often as they could, stealing stolen moments of fleeting happiness in the secluded gardens of the palace, their love more potent than ever before.

"I am yours, Safwan," Aurya whispered one fateful night, as they lay entwined beneath the silvery moonlight. "Forever and always, my heart belongs to you."

"And mine to yours, my Gem," he responded, his voice thick with emotion. "This life, and the next, and all the ones to follow."

As the sun rose on the day of her wedding, Aurya bade a tearful farewell to Safwan, their hands clasped together through the bars of her carriage, their scorching gaze a silent promise that their love would endure.

With a final, heart-wrenching squeeze, their fingers slid apart, and Aurya turned to face her destiny as the bride of a man she did not love. But her heart, and her soul, would always belong to the prince who had stolen her heart that fateful day in the marketplace.

The early years of Aurya's marriage to the emir's son were fraught with tension and unease. Though he treated her with the utmost respect and courtesy, there was a distance between them that no amount of time or shared experiences could bridge.

As the years passed, Aurya's life in the emir's court settled into a familiar routine. Her days were filled with the duties expected of a highborn lady, and her nights were spent in the sprawling, empty halls of her new home, her heart aching for the love she had left behind. Safwan, too, had married a woman of his family's choosing, and try as they might, the distance between them seemed to grow wider with each passing season.

One evening, as Aurya wandered the gardens of her new home, her heart heavy with longing, she stumbled upon an old woman tending to the manor's fig trees. There was an other-worldly air about her, an aura of power and wisdom that transcended her wrinkled skin and stooped posture.

"My lady," the old woman said, not looking up from her work, "I know the burden you carry in your heart."

Startled, Aurya turned to face the woman, whose eyes, when she finally looked up, were as ancient as the stars themselves.

"You seek a way to be with your true love, the prince from afar," the woman continued, her voice cracked with age but carrying a weight that brooked no denial. "I can help you, if you are prepared to pay the price."

Aurya's heart leaped in her chest. Could it be that Fate had finally dealt her a kind hand? She gazed into the old woman's depthless eyes, and in that moment, she knew her decision had been made.

"I will pay any price, my lady," she vowed, dropping to her knees before the old woman. "Show me the way."

The old woman's lips curled into a cryptic smile, and she extended a gnarled hand towards the rising moon. "Then swear an oath, by the light of La Luna, that you will give whatever is asked of you to ensure your love's unending embrace."

Without hesitation, Aurya took the old woman's hand, and in that moment, their fates were sealed. The moonlight bathed them both, and as they swore their solemn oaths, the night echoed with the rustling of a hundred thousand wings.

Aurya's heart pounded like a wild animal in her chest as she crept through the shadowy alleyways, her silk gown rustling with each cautious step. The full moon cast a pale light on the cobblestone streets, casting long, ominous shadows that seemed to reach out to her. Fear slithered down her spine, but her determination to be with Safwan outweighed her trepidation. These were the steps

Jasmine incense wafted through the air, overpowering the stench of the dank alley, and Aurya knew she had reached her destination. The crumbling facade of Zahra al-Majid's abode seemed to loom over her, as if the very building were a sentient witness to her forbidden desires. With a shaking hand, she rapped thrice on the splintered wooden door.

The door creaked open, and a bony hand beckoned her inside. A chill ran down Aurya's spine, but she steeled herself and crossed the threshold into the sorceress's lair.

Candles flickered in the dimly lit antechamber, casting flickering shadows on the walls. A low, throbbing chant emanated from the depths of the house, and Aurya's courage wavered.

"Speak your thoughts, child," a voice seemingly said from all around her. "I know why you have come."

Aurya swallowed her fear. "I am here to beg for your help, Zahra al-Majid. I love a man who is not mine to love, yet my heart will not allow me to be with any other."

Zahra appeared before her, seemingly out of thin air, her inscrutable gaze boring into Aurya's very soul. "And what would you be willing to give, O daughter of the Caliph, to bind your heart to his?"

Aurya's breath caught in her throat, but she knew the stakes. "Anything," she whispered, her voice barely a whisper.

"So be it," Zahra cackled, her laughter echoing off the crumbling walls. "You shall have your heart's desire, but know this: the price you pay will be steep, and the consequences eternal."

Aurya's stomach churned, but she could not back down now. She knelt before the sorceress, her skirts pooling on the dusty floor. "I am ready. Tell me what must be done."

Zahra's eyes glowed with an unearthly light, and she began to list the sacrifices Aurya must make. A shiver ran down Aurya's spine as she realized the magnitude of her choice, but her love for Safwan was all-consuming.

"First, you must give me the life of your twin brother," Zahra intoned, her voice cold as death.

Aurya's heart nearly stopped, but she nodded, tears streaming down her cheeks. "It is done."

"Then, pluck out your own eye and mix it with the blood of a white stallion."

Aurya winced, but steeling herself, she plucked out her right eye, wincing as the world went blurry. "I-I have done it."

"Lastly, swallow this," Zahra said, holding out a vial of viscous black liquid. "And you shall feel the pain of a thousand burning suns, as your very essence is bound to his."

Aurya took the vial, her trembling hand spilling drops onto her dress. She could feel the potion searing her skin, but she lifted it to her lips and gulped the contents down.

The pain that followed was unbearable, as if the fires of Jannah consumed her from within. A scream tore from her lips, but she remained kneeling, eyes wide with agony.

As the sun rose, Zahra's cackling faded, leaving Aurya alone with the rotting carcass of her steed and the prospect of the lifeless body of her twin brother. Blood stained her hands and gown, and one eye socket wept blood. Aurya hobbled home, her body aching and her soul shattered, but her love for Safwan remained unshaken.

Days passed like centuries, and Aurya's anticipation grew. Finally, the night of the new moon arrived. A hooded figure with a familiar gait slipped into her chambers.

"Aurya," Safwan breathed, relief in his voice. "I've missed you so much."

Joy filled her heart, replacing the icy void that had taken root. "I've yearned for this moment too," she whispered, "but... there is something I must show you."

With a graceful gesture, she let her hood fall away, revealing her ruined visage. Safwan recoiled, his eyes wide with horror.

"My love, what have you done?"

Aurya's heart shattered. "For you, Safwan. I would move the heavens and earth themselves for our love."

Safwan's expression softened, but Aurya saw the truth in his eyes. He had never loved her as she had him. It was then that the full weight of her actions crashed down upon her. The death of her brother, her disfigurement, and the curse of immortality... all for a love that was not hers to claim.

Despair welled within her, as dark as the depths of the ocean.

"I... I cannot," Safwan stammered, taking a step back. "I... I'm sorry."

Aurya's broken heart shattered further. "No, Safwan, please! I can fix this! I'll undo it all!"

But it was too late. Safwan had made his choice. With a shout of rage, Aurya lunged at him, sinking her newly sharpened teeth into his neck.

Warmth flooded her mouth, and for a fleeting moment, she tasted redemption. Safwan's cries of terror faded into the ether, replaced by the rush of power coursing through her veins.

The sun rose, casting its golden light upon the bloodied chamber, illuminating the handsome prince's lifeless body and the monstrous creature kneeling over him.

Aurya, the once fair maiden, had become a monster. Her right eye now returned.

Her heart ached with the weight of her new reality. She was no longer human, but a creature of darkness and despair. The taste of immortality had replaced the sweetness of love, and she was left with nothing but the bitter aftertaste. The sun rose, casting its golden light upon the bloodied chamber, illuminating the handsome prince's lifeless body and the monstrous creature kneeling over him.

Aurya, the once fair maiden, had become a monster. Her right eye now returned, glowing with a crimson hue that mirrored her tormented soul. She could feel the curse of immortality pulsating within her veins, a constant reminder of the bargain she had made with the sorceress Zahra.

As the sun dipped below the horizon, casting shadows over the rocky cliffs, Aurya knew she could not bear the torment any longer. She needed to end her suffering, and if she could not undo the curse, she would take her own life.

In the distance, Safwan's resting place was being prepared. But as she stood at the edge of the cliff, staring down at the jagged rocks below, Aurya felt a sudden surge of power. It was the same power that had filled her when she drank Safwan's blood, and she knew that it was a taste of the immortality she craved.

With a cry of anguish, she leaped from the cliff, her body plummeting toward the sea below. The wind rushed past her as she fell, and for a fleeting moment, she thought she could see Safwan's smiling face in the clouds.

But just as she was about to hit the water, she vanished. In an instant, she had become a shadow, rushing through the night like a whirlwind. She was free from the constraints of her body, free from the curse of immortality, and free from the love that had defined her existence.

Back in the village, amid the preparations for Safwan's burial, something strange began to happen. As the moon rose, a soft light began to emanate from the prince's body. It was a glow that seemed to defy the very laws of nature, and those who watched could not help but feel a sense of awe and reverence.

Suddenly, Safwan's body began to stir. There was no sign of death in his countenance, only a look of wonder and determination.

The weight of his second chance hung heavy on his shoulders. He couldn't shake the feeling that it was unnatural, almost like a curse. But at the same time, he couldn't deny the opportunity to save Aurya, to right the wrongs of their past. His mind and heart were at war, unsure of what was truly the right path to take.

Chapter 2

طوفان "Flood"

Paris in the 1910s was a city of contrasts, where the grandeur of the Eiffel Tower cast long shadows over the cobblestone streets and the Seine whispered secrets under its many bridges. Aurya Alcazar moved through the City of Light like a phantom from another era, her raven-black hair billowing softly behind her as the vibrant art scene embraced her with open arms, unaware of the darkness that dwelled within her ethereal beauty.

The bourgeoisie welcomed her with gilded invitations to salons filled with the scent of oil paint and the clinking of champagne glasses, their laughter echoing through opulent halls. Safwan, his regal bearing never diminishing despite the centuries, followed in her wake, a silent guardian whose eyes held the weight of an undying sorrow.

As night fell upon Paris, the city transformed into an enchanting labyrinth of flickering gaslights and hushed alleyways. It was here that Aurya's true nature unfurled like the petals of a nocturnal bloom. She stalked the shadows with a predator's grace, her dark eyes reflecting the pale moonlight as she honed in on her unsuspecting prey—a lone figure ambling home after a soirée.

Safwan watched from a distance, his heart heavy with a mix of disgust and concern. With every step Aurya took towards the oblivious Parisian, he felt the chasm between them widen. There was an elegance, a seductive dance to her movements; yet each gesture was a reminder of the curse they shared.

He could see the briefest moment of hesitation in Aurya's stance before she struck, swift and silent as the grave. Her victim's final breath was a mere sigh in the cool night air, a secret carried away by the wind. He observed as she drew back, her lips stained with life, her face alight with a hunger sated. The thrill of the hunt had awakened something primal within her, and Safwan knew that with each drop of blood she consumed, Aurya was becoming more comfortable with the monster she had become.

And yet, as Aurya turned to him, her gaze searching for approval or perhaps absolution, Safwan felt the pull of their bond, an inescapable tether tying his fate to hers. In her eyes, glimmering with the remnants of her feast, there was also vulnerability—a silent plea for understanding that transcended the horrors of their existence.

Their walk back through the lamplit streets was a silent procession, the tension palpable as they returned to the façade of civility amongst the artistic elite. Safwan's thoughts churned like the dark waters of the Seine, knowing that this city, alive with creativity and passion, was now also a witness to their eternal struggle for power over their own cursed natures.

In the quiet of their shared quarters, as the distant echo of a jazz band played into the early hours, Safwan contemplated the woman he loved. Aurya, once a noblewoman of al-Andalus, now a creature of shadow and thirst. And himself, a prince turned pariah, forever bound to the night. As Aurya retreated to solitude, leaving Safwan alone amidst the opulence that felt more like a gilded cage, the rain began to fall on Paris, like tears for the immortality that both united and divided them.

The chandelier's crystals cast fragmented light across the salon, where Paris' elite mingled in a symphony of silk and whispers. Aurya Alcazar, draped in sapphire velvet that clung to her like the shadows of dusk, navigated the throng with the ease of eternity on her side. Her laughter—a melody spun from the dark recesses of centuries—enchanted the artists and merchants alike. The tales of her wealth as a merchant, trading in rare commodities that seemed to defy time itself, were woven into every conversation, each anecdote more extravagant than the last.

"Mademoiselle Alcazar," a baroness cooed, clutching a bejeweled hand to her chest, "your taste is impeccable. To think such treasures could be found!"

"Time affords one a certain... discernment," Aurya replied, her gaze lingering on the pulsing veins of the gathered aristocracy.

A figure detached from the shadows, his noble bearing unmistakable even amid the gaudy splendor of the nouveau riche. Safwan's eyes, two flints sparking in the dim light, locked onto Aurya. He moved through the crowd, a specter of a forgotten era, until he stood before her, their silent communication a private affair amidst public opulence.

"Must you revel in this charade?" Safwan murmured once they stood alone on a balcony overlooking the rain-slicked streets. Below them, Paris thrived, unknowing and ripe.

"Charade?" Aurya's laugh was sharp, a shard of glass wrapped in velvet. "This is survival, Safwan. Our survival."

"Feeding on the innocent, Aurya? There are other ways—"

"Are there?" She turned her back to him, looking out over the city that had embraced her darkness with open arms. "You speak of innocence as though it were an unspoiled fruit in Eden. But we are far from Eden, my love."

Safwan recoiled, the word 'love' striking deeper than any fang. "We can be better than our curse. We can choose—"

"Choose?" Aurya spun around, her expression fierce, her beauty terrible in its wrath. "You speak of choice when we are bound by chains not of our making? I take what little power is offered to me, Safwan. If immortality has taught me anything, it is that."

"Power taken at the expense of life is despotism, not freedom," Safwan countered, his voice rising above the whisper of rain against stone.

"Then let me be a despot!" Aurya declared, her words slicing through the humid air between them. "For centuries, I have been a pawn in the games of men, of fate. No longer."

Their gazes locked in a battle as old as their undead hearts—the struggle for dominance, for righteousness, for a semblance of the humanity they once knew. Aurya's eyes blazed with a fire that belied the coldness of her skin, while Safwan's simmered with a sorrow that no amount of time could quench.

"Where does this path lead us, Aurya?" Safwan pleaded, the prince in him reaching for the noblewoman she once was.

"Forward," she said simply, her voice softening for a moment. "Always forward, for that is the only direction left to us."

As the night deepened and the lights of Paris flickered like distant stars, the space between Aurya and Safwan stretched taut, filled with the echoes of a love that refused to yield to the darkness yet struggled to find the light.

Rain lashed against the windowpanes of their Parisian apartment, the drops like insistent fingers tapping a morse code of foreboding. Inside, shadows clung to the corners, shrouding the opulent room in an air of tension that seemed almost suffocating. Aurya stood by the fireplace, her reflection in the darkened mirror above it distorted by the play of flickering candlelight. Her eyes, pools of liquid darkness, were fixed upon Safwan, who paced the length of the Persian rug with the caged restlessness of a beast.

"Must you pace so?" Aurya's voice sliced through the patter of the rain, sharp and cold as the blade of a guillotine. "It is like being trapped with a nervous animal."

Safwan stopped, turning toward her abruptly, his expression tormented. "I can no longer bear this, Aurya. This... feeding on innocents while pretending to be something we are not. It gnaws at me."

"Then perhaps it is you who should adapt," she retorted, her tone laden with centuries of suppressed rage. "Our nature is our strength, Safwan. We are superior to these fragile mortals."

"Superior?" Safwan's voice was a low growl, tinged with disgust. "What vanity has immortality whispered into your ear? We are but leeches living off the blood of others."

"Leeches?" The word hung between them, charged with accusation. Aurya stepped forward, her movements graceful yet predatory. "We are gods among insects. My influence grows because I accept what we are. I embrace the power that comes with our curse."

"Is that what you see?" Safwan swept his arm towards the rain-streaked window. "A world to dominate? Our curse is penance, not privilege. And you, Aurya, you revel in it!"

"Revel?" A low laugh escaped her lips, a sound devoid of joy. "I do not revel, I survive. And I will not apologize for refusing to live in the shadows, to skulk in shame. If you cannot stomach our existence, then perhaps it is you who does not belong."

"Belong?" The word echoed, a remnant of some long-lost plea for belonging. Safwan's face hardened, his princely features set in a mask of resolve. "I belong to a time when honor meant something. When love was more than an excuse for barbarity."

"Love?" Aurya spat the word out as if it were poison. "You speak of love, yet you question my every move. You hold me back, Safwan, chain me to your antiquated morals!"

"Chain you?" His reply came soft, a whisper against the storm outside. "No, Aurya. It is you who are chained—chained to a past you refuse to release, to a hunger you cannot control."

"Control?" She advanced on him now, her voice rising like the crescendo of the tempest beyond the walls. "You dare speak to me of control? I have mastered myself, while you whimper over the nature of our sustenance!"

Safwan's eyes blazed with a fire that matched her own. "To master oneself is not to indulge every impulse, but to rise above them. You are no master, Aurya. You are a slave to your desires."

"Enough!" Aurya's outcry reverberated through the room, and for a moment, the rain seemed to hush in deference. "If you cannot stand beside me, then stand apart. But do not presume to dictate how I wield the gift of eternity."

Safwan shook his head, the sorrow returning to his eyes as he looked upon her, the woman he had loved through lifetimes. "This is no gift—it is our shared damnation. And I fear, Aurya, that in your quest for power, you may lose yourself completely."

The words hung heavy in the air, laden with an ancient grief that neither time nor immortality could erase. As the rain continued to pour, the space between them grew wider—a chasm filled with the echoes of their immortal agony.

Rain lashed against the expansive windows of the Parisian apartment, its rhythm a relentless reminder of the world outside—a world that Aurya had taken as her own. Inside, the tempest raged not just beyond the glass but also within the gilded walls that contained two beings bound by an eternity far crueler than any storm.

"Is this what we have become?" Safwan's voice was barely audible above the downpour, a strained whisper that bore the weight of centuries. His silhouette, outlined against the darkened room, seemed to waver as if it might dissolve into the shadows that played upon the rich tapestries and antique furnishings of their abode.

"Have we?" Aurya spat back, the fire in her eyes undimmed by the creeping dampness that seemed to seep through every crevice. "Or is it just you who cannot stomach the truth of our existence?"

"Truth?" Safwan echoed, his gaze fixing on her with a pained intensity. "What truth? That we are condemned to a life of predation? To forever feed on the innocence of those who still possess what we have lost?"

"Lost?" The word fell from her lips like a curse, heavy with scorn. "We have lost nothing. We have gained power, beauty, eternity! Yet you squander it on futile dreams of redemption."

"Redemption..." Safwan's voice faltered, and for a moment, he seemed to crumble under the burden of his own despair. "Can there be happiness for us, Aurya? Is there joy to be found in this ceaseless night?"

Aurya's laugh was a sharp, bitter sound that cut through the air like a blade. "You speak of joy when we are gods among mortals?"

"Gods do not bleed," Safwan murmured, turning away from her piercing gaze. "Nor do they feel the pangs of conscience that torment me so."

"Then perhaps it is your conscience that has betrayed you, not I." Her words were a venomous hiss, each syllable dripping with accusation and disdain.

Safwan flinched, as though struck, his eyes closing briefly against the onslaught. When he opened them again, they were filled with a sorrow deeper than the ocean that once caressed the shores of their lost homeland.

"Perhaps," he conceded, his voice barely above a whisper, "it is we who have betrayed ourselves."

The silence that followed was suffocating, broken only by the relentless drumming of the rain against the windowpanes. It was a symphony of nature's indifference to the turmoil of those who walked the earth untouched by time.

Aurya drew herself up, her posture regal, yet tinged with the ferocity of a creature cornered. "I am done with this," she declared, her voice resonating with finality. "Done with your doubts, your fears, your pathetic yearning for a humanity that is no longer ours."

Without another word, she turned on her heel, her movements fluid and graceful, yet underscored by an anger that seemed to radiate from her very being. She swept toward the door, her figure cutting through the oppressive atmosphere like a ship forging ahead through stormy seas.

"Where will you go?" Safwan asked, though he already knew the answer.

"Wherever I please," Aurya retorted without looking back, her hand grasping the doorknob with a resolve that spoke of an unyielding will. The door swung open, and she stepped into the tempest, the cold embrace of the Parisian night swallowing her whole.

The door closed with a resounding thud behind her, leaving Safwan alone amidst the echoes of their confrontation. The rain continued its relentless assault on the city, indifferent to the heartache and uncertainty that now enveloped him like a shroud.

He stood motionless, a solitary figure engulfed by the opulence of a room that suddenly felt as vast and empty as the centuries stretching before him. In the gloom, the ghosts of their argument lingered, haunting whispers that questioned the very essence of their bond.

"Can there be happiness for us?" The question hung in the air, unanswered, as Safwan contemplated a future fraught with the complexities of immortality—a future now uncertain as the path Aurya had chosen to walk alone.

Safwan's eyes lingered on the closed door, a barrier as formidable as the one now between his heart and Aurya's. He felt the pull of their centuries-old love, a force as undeniable as the gravity that bound him to this accursed earth. Yet, it was his unwavering moral compass, forged in the fires of his princely duties, that now weighed upon him like chains. Each drop of rain that pattered against the windowpane echoed the rhythm of his internal conflict—persistence or surrender, love or righteousness.

In the shadow-strewn corners of the lavish apartment, where art and luxury intertwined, Safwan wrestled with the torment of eternity. With every life taken by their kind, a piece of his soul seemed to wither, leaving behind a hollow echo of the noble man he once was. The weight of immortality pressed upon him, a relentless reminder of the never-ending cycle of nightfall and dawn, each bringing forth trials that tested the limits of his resolve.

Outside, the Parisian night unfurled before Aurya like a canvas awaiting her brush. She moved through the rain-soaked streets, her form a spectral presence against the backdrop of flickering street lamps and glistening cobblestones. The city's vibrant pulse called to her vampiric nature, a siren song that stirred both excitement and an underlying sense of isolation within her ageless heart.

The rain fell upon her, droplets weaving through her raven-black hair like liquid silver, but she did not seek shelter. Instead, she embraced the deluge, letting it cleanse away the heated words and smoldering anger that had driven her from the sanctuary of their shared abode. The freedom she found in this stormy embrace brought with it an intoxicating rush, yet the absence of Safwan's steady presence carved a void that even the tempest could not fill.

Aurya's stride was purposeful as she navigated the labyrinthine alleys, her keen eyes capturing glimpses of mortal lives that flared brightly and then faded, reminding her of her own ceaseless journey through the corridors of time. The thrill of independence warred with the pang of solitude, each step away from Safwan a testament to her fierce desire for autonomy and the unspoken fear that she may have forsaken the only one who truly understood the depths of her eternal struggle.

Back in the confines of their residence, Safwan remained still, his gaze fixed on the void left by Aurya's departure. The relentless downpour outside mirrored the tumult in his heart—a storm that showed no sign of abating. His love for Aurya was a beacon that had guided him through the darkest nights, but now, even that light was obscured by the maelstrom of his principles.

And so they stood, divided by choices and ideals, united by a bond that defied time itself—a prince ensnared by honor, and a noblewoman caught in the throes of emancipation. Both adrift in a world that offered them eternity, yet robbed them of the solace found in life's fleeting nature.

The rain outside had turned savage, a torrential cascade that seemed intent on washing away the very stones of Paris. Within the apartment, Safwan sat motionless, the echoes of Aurya's departure hanging heavy in the air, as tangible as the antique tapestries that adorned the walls. The weight of centuries pressed upon his shoulders, a burden of endless nights and blood-stained dawns.

His mind wandered through the labyrinth of their shared past, each memory a shard of glass glistening with the blood of sacrifices made. Once, they had reveled in the gift of immortality, dancing through the ages with abandon. But time had eroded that joy, leaving a chasm between them, filled with the souls of those they had consumed to sustain their cursed existence.

A flicker of lightning illuminated the room, casting spectral shadows that danced like wraiths across Safwan's face. He pondered the countless faces that had blurred into obscurity, the lives extinguished by their insatiable thirst. With every life taken, a piece of their humanity had been surrendered, until he wondered what remained beneath the surface of their ageless façades.

Lost in these somber reflections, Safwan barely registered the click of the door latch or the soft squelch of wet fabric. It was only when a gust of wind ushered in the scent of rain and jasmine—the fragrance that clung to Aurya like a whispered secret—that he roused from his reverie.

Aurya stood in the doorway, her silhouette framed by the tumultuous night beyond. Rivulets of water traced the graceful lines of her face, dripping from her lashes like the tears of a goddess. Her cloak, once vibrant, now clung to her form, a sodden testament to her flight through the storm.

"Paris weeps for us," she murmured, her voice a blend of defiance and despair that echoed the thunder outside.

Safwan's gaze met hers, finding the tempest within her eyes had quieted, giving way to a clarity that pierced him sharper than any blade. In that moment, the remnants of anger that had fueled her departure seemed to dissolve, replaced by an unspoken admission of her own vulnerability.

"Perhaps," Safwan replied, his words measured, "it is we who weep for ourselves—for what we have become."

A shiver, born not of cold but of recognition, passed through Aurya as she stepped inside, shedding the cloak that bore the storm's embrace. She moved closer, and Safwan could see the subtle shift in her demeanor, the softening at the edges of her immortal mask.

"Immortality," she started, pausing to choose her words with care, "is a lonely road, paved with intentions both noble and vile. Yet, I find the path less daunting with you beside me."

In the silence that followed, the resonance of her confession lingered, a fragile bridge spanning the distance their argument had wrought. The rain continued its relentless symphony against the windowpanes, indifferent to the reconciliation unfolding within the dimly lit room.

"Can we ever be free?" Safwan found himself asking, his voice barely above a whisper, a question meant for them both.

"Freedom," Aurya said, closing the gap between them, her hands tentatively reaching for his, "is as much a prison as this eternity we share. But perhaps together, we can find solace amidst the chaos."

They stood there, two ancient souls clinging to the remnants of their humanity, as the storm raged on, indifferent to the plight of those who had transcended time, yet remained ensnared by its cruel machinations.

Safwan's gaze met Aurya's as they stood enveloped in the aftermath of their tempestuous dispute. The walls of their Parisian apartment, once a sanctuary from the world's prying eyes, seemed to press inwards with oppressive weight, bearing witness to the fractures in their eternal bond.

"Every epoch we traverse," Safwan breathed, his voice threading through the tension that hung like drapery between them, "we face the same fears, the same desires. Yet, here we remain, perpetual strangers to death and its finality."

Aurya's eyes, dark mirrors reflecting centuries of sorrow and fleeting joy, held his gaze as if drinking in his very soul. "Do you ever tire, my love, of this endless masquerade? To be forever chasing horizons that retreat as we advance?"

He felt her vulnerability, raw and unshielding, a rare glimpse into the chasm within her heart. It was a chasm he knew all too well, for it mirrored his own—a pit dug by years of existence without the sweet release of oblivion.

"Each dawn I rise," she whispered, "I do so with the weight of countless dusks upon my shoulders. Our every step is etched with the echoes of lives we've touched – and taken."

"Is there no respite, Aurya?" The question lingered, a specter of doubt in the charged air.

"Perhaps not," she conceded, her voice softening with a weariness that belied her immortal facade. "But in this relentless pursuit, we have yet discovered moments... Moments where time yields, and we are merely two souls intertwined by fate's cruel hand."

The rain outside persisted in its lullaby, a rhythmic reminder of life's constant flow, indifferent to those who stood outside its cycle. And in that moment, as they reached for each other, their hands clasped like two parts of a severed whole seeking reunion, they found solace.

Within the circle of Safwan's arms, Aurya allowed herself to feel the warmth that had long since become a distant memory. His embrace was both fortress and bastion against the night that raged beyond their haven. In the strength of his hold, she sensed not just the power that coursed through his veins but also the tenderness of a love that had refused to yield to time's relentless march.

"Here," Safwan murmured, his lips grazing her forehead, anointing her with a kiss that spoke of eons, "here in the eye of our storm, we find refuge."

"Amidst the chaos," Aurya replied, her voice a mere breath against his chest, "our love endures."

As the downpour outside painted the world anew, washing away the sins of a city lost to nocturnal excess, Aurya and

Safwan reclaimed each other. They clung not to the illusions of the past nor to the uncertainty of the future, but to the undeniable truth of their now—two immortal beings whose hearts beat as one within the passage of ceaseless rain.

The silence between them grew, a living entity in the dimly lit apartment. Shadows cast by the flickering candles danced upon the walls, mimicking the tumultuous emotions that ebbed and flowed through the room. Rain lashed against the windows with unrelenting ferocity, the sound a constant reminder of the tempest not only outside but also within their hearts.

Aurya stared into the dark void beyond the glass, her mind adrift amidst the storm. The streets of Paris, washed clean by heaven's tears, mirrored her turbulent thoughts. Safwan watched her, his eyes reflecting a war of conflicting desires—a longing to reach out and mend what was broken, yet restrained by the knowledge that some fractures ran too deep for simple repair.

"Will we ever find peace?" he asked, voice barely above a whisper, yet it cut through the silence as a sword through silk.

Auryan turned from the window, her gaze piercing him with an intensity that spoke volumes. "Peace is a mortal conceit," she said, her tone carrying the weight of centuries. "We are eternally caught in the throes of our own making, my love."

"Is this all there is then? An eternity of struggle?" Safwan's question hung in the air, heavy with doubt.

"Perhaps," Aurya conceded, her lips curving into a mirthless smile. "But even gods grow weary of omnipotence. Power without purpose is a hollow victory, and immortality without connection is a sentence we serve together."

Safwan moved closer, the distance between them now merely physical. "And what of loyalty? To each other?" he pressed, seeking an anchor in the vast sea of their existence.

"Loyalty..." Aurya mused, turning back to the rain-smeared window. Her reflection, ghostly and transient, seemed to merge with the night. "It is both our compass and our chain. But where it leads us, that remains to be seen."

His hand reached for hers, a lifeline thrown across the chasm that yawned open at their feet. Their fingers touched, a fleeting connection that promised so much more, yet it was as fragile as the last leaf clinging to a winter branch.

"Then let us step into the unknown together," Safwan declared, though his voice betrayed the tremble of one who knew the path would not always be kind.

A single nod from Aurya sealed their silent pact, yet the commitment was fractured, like light refracting through a prism—beautiful but scattered in a myriad of directions.

As the clock chimed the hour, its mournful toll echoed the sentiment of their hearts. Time was both ally and adversary, a paradox they could never escape. With a final glance at the man beside her, Aurya drew away from his embrace and crossed the room, her movements shadowed with ambiguity.

The night continued unabated, oblivious to the two immortal souls within the Parisian apartment who grappled with the gravity of their undying love and the specter of the unknown that lay ahead. And as the rain whispered secrets to the cobblestones below, Aurya and Safwan faced the dawn of a new century with a fractured commitment, bound by love yet divided by fate.

Chapter 3

كسر "Fracture

The moon hung low over the ancient cliffs of al-Andalus, its light casting long shadows that danced upon the fortress walls. Within those stone confines, Safwan's anguished cries echoed into the night, a symphony of torment that only the ceaseless waves dared to answer. The prince, once regal and resolute, now lay prostrate on the cold floor, his chest heaving with each ragged breath as the cruel gift of immortality coursed through his veins.

"Curse this wretched existence," he rasped, his voice a mere whisper against the cacophony of his despair. Aurya stood at the precipice of their shared damnation, her silhouette a stark contrast against the luminescent glow that bathed her in ethereal light. She reached out, her hand trembling as she longed to offer solace, but Safwan recoiled, his eyes—a tempest of sorrow and accusation—locking onto hers.

"Was our love so feeble that you would tether me to this endless void?" His words lashed out like whips, each syllable weighted with the bitterness that festered within his soul.

Aurya's heart fractured anew at the sight of her beloved reduced to such a state. "I sought to preserve us, not to imprison you," she replied, her own voice a haunting melody of regret. Yet the distance between them spanned more than the mere inches of desolate space; it was an abyss wrought from choices that could never be undone.

Paris in the 1910s unfurled its splendor before them like a tapestry woven from threads of gaiety and opulence. But beneath the city's vibrant facade, there lurked a current of malice that whispered of forbidden unions and unnatural beings. Aurya and Safwan, draped in the finery befitting their masquerade as wealthy merchants, navigated the cobblestone streets with a grace that belied their inner turmoil.

To the Parisian elite, they were exotic enigmas, their accents tinged with the mystery of distant lands. Yet behind every admiring gaze and cordial smile, suspicion festered. Their love, an intricate dance amidst the flames of prejudice, found no sanctuary even amidst the glittering salons and smoke-filled cabarets.

"Even here, we are but phantoms flitting through the lives of mortals," Safwan murmured one evening as they watched the Seine reflect the city's lights, a river of stars amidst the darkness.

"Perhaps it is time we seek refuge elsewhere," Aurya suggested, her voice barely rising above the din of the soirée that teemed around them. "Our presence invites peril, and Paris grows weary of our charade."

"Ever the nomads of time, my Gem," Safwan conceded, the endearment spoken with a tenderness that momentarily dispelled the clouds of his discontent. He offered her his arm, a gesture of unity against a world that would never understand the complexity of their existence.

With a nod sealed in silent agreement, they turned their backs on the City of Light, its allure fading into memory like the last glimmers of twilight surrendering to the encroaching night. Ahead lay the unknown, a path shrouded in the mist of centuries yet traveled, their immortal journey an eternal testament to the power struggles and loyalties that both bound and divided them.

In the solitude of their departure, Aurya and Safwan faced the unyielding truth: no matter where they roamed, the specter of immortality would forever haunt their steps, a phantom witness to the undying love that both condemned and redeemed them.

Rain lashed at the paper walls of the old mountain home, where Aurya and Safwan found solace from the relentless downpour. The typhoon raged outside, a furious testament to nature's untamed power, mirroring the tempest that had long brewed within their own immortal hearts. Cloistered within this wooden sanctuary, they sat across from Laila Omar, whose eyes sparkled like lanterns in the storm, promising warmth and perhaps, a path to absolution.

"Redemption is not a port you can sail to," Laila spoke with serene conviction as she poured steaming tea into delicate porcelain cups. "It is a journey through uncharted waters." Her words danced through the air, resonating with the wisdom of ages, even as the rain drummed an incessant beat upon the roof.

Aurya leaned forward, her raven-black hair spilling around her shoulders like ink against the backdrop of her pale brown skin. "And how does one navigate such a voyage?" she asked, her voice a haunting melody tinged with hope.

"By understanding the currents that drive you," replied Laila, her own gaze steady upon the couple. She handed them each a cup, the steam curling upwards like spirits in communion.

The next day, under a reluctant sun peeking through retreating clouds, the trio ventured into town. The streets bustled with life, yet the air hung heavy with the scent of change. Japan was on the cusp of modernity, its economic heartbeat quickening after the Great War's demand for industry and innovation.

As they walked, Aurya sensed the wary glances of townsfolk, their eyes flickering with superstition. The war had brought prosperity, but it had also awakened fears of shadows that moved in tandem with the light. In hushed tones, Laila recounted the whispers that clung to the cobblestones like morning mist.

"Dark times are seen by dark creatures," she said. "And some believe you carry the darkness with you."

Safwan's jaw tightened imperceptibly, his regal posture a shield against the murmurs of ill omens. He knew all too well the burden of misjudged appearances, of judgments cast by those who could never comprehend the depths of his existence.

"Let them think what they will," Safwan declared, though his heart ached with the familiar sting of rejection. "We are beyond their reach."

"Are we?" Aurya questioned softly, her expressive eyes reflecting the pain of centuries spent skirting the fringes of humanity.

"Perhaps," Laila interjected gently, "it is not about escaping their reach, but about bridging the expanse between fear and understanding."

Amidst the ebb and flow of a society grappling with its identity, Aurya, Safwan, and Laila moved like specters from another age, their presence a silent echo of the past that whispered through the present. And as they withdrew from the town's watchful gaze, returning to the seclusion of their mountain abode, the promise of a dawn filled with clearer skies and quieter seas lingered on the horizon—a beacon of hope in the ceaseless night of immortality.

Under a bruised sky, swollen with the threat of another typhoon, Aurya and Safwan tread softly through the dense underbrush, their senses attuned to the silent symphony of nature. The nocturnal world was alive around them, a stark contrast to the stillness within their own eternal hearts. It was Laila's counsel that led them here, beneath the boughs of whispering trees, to seek sustenance from creatures of the forest rather than the souls of men.

"Remember," Laila's words echoed in Aurya's mind, "to take only what you must to survive." But as fangs pierced flesh and life ebbed into their mouths, their actions remained unseen yet not unfelt in the tapestry of the living.

In the days that followed, the mountainside whispered secrets of its own, tales of livestock found cold and pale at dawn. Wounds, precise as moonlit shadows, marred the necks of the fallen animals. Whispers swirled among the townsfolk like leaves in the wind—fearful, accusatory, a growing storm of suspicion.

One dusk, as crimson seeped across the sky, painting the world in shades of fire and blood, the villagers, armed with anger and rusted scythes, ascended the treacherous path to the abode they deemed cursed. Laila's hut, perched precariously on the mountainside, became the heart of an unfolding tragedy.

"Let us face them!" Safwan hissed, the warrior prince within him rising like a tempest, ready to unleash centuries of pent-up fury. His hand reached for the hilt of an invisible sword, a gesture born from instinct and ages of conflict.

Aurya's voice cut through the chaos like a sharp blade, her words dripping with disdain. "You are so foolish, Safwan," she spat, silencing the impending violence with her venomous words.

Laila stood at the threshold, the embodiment of serenity against the backdrop of chaos. "Peace," she urged, her eyes pools of resolve. "Your struggle is not with them, but with the curse that binds you."

"Go now, into the night," Laila commanded, as she turned to face the torches that bobbed like angry spirits making their ascent. "Find the peace I cannot give you here."

Aurya and Safwan, bound by love stronger than the chains of immortality, hesitated. Their hearts drummed a mournful dirge, a requiem for the choice being made. Yet, as the mob encroached, spewing vitriol and fear, they knew Laila's sacrifice would be their deliverance or their damnation.

"Forgive us," they murmured in unison, stepping back into the shadows that had long been their refuge.

The townspeople arrived, breathless from the climb, hearts fueled by a fervor that could not be quenched. They found Laila alone, her silhouette defiant against the flames that soon rose to claim her.

"Witch!" they cried out, their voices a single entity of wrath and righteousness. Flames licked the night sky, casting a lurid glow over faces twisted with triumph and terror alike.

Laila's gaze never wavered, even as the fire embraced her. Her final words, carried on the smoke that curled upwards, were a benediction for those who fled and a lament for those who could not see beyond the veil of their own fears.

"Be free," she whispered, and the stars themselves seemed to pause in their celestial dance.

And so, under a canopy of grief and starlight, Aurya and Safwan vanished into the embrace of the night, the echoes of Laila's sacrifice reverberating in their immortal souls, a haunting melody of love and loss entwined.

Chapter 4

تسربل بالعار

"Crowded"

The taxi door swung open, and Aurya Alcazar emerged like a specter from another era into the pulsing heart of Manhattan. The city's vibrant energy enveloped her, the cacophony of honking horns and chattering pedestrians a stark contrast to the serene hush of al-Andalusian waves she once knew so well. Beside her, Prince Safwan stepped onto the sidewalk, his noble bearing unfazed by the chaos that swirled around them.

Together, they stood on the edge of possibility, their immortal gaze sweeping over the towering edifices that clawed at the sky. The very air of the 1960s New York City seemed electric with promise, charged with the dreams of a million souls. Aurya inhaled deeply, the myriad scents of the city—exhaust fumes mixed with street vendor aromas—filling her lungs, reminding her that though they were creatures of the night, the world belonged as much to them as it did to the mortals who bustled past.

They moved through the throngs of people, Aurya's raven-black hair and ethereal pallor drawing covert glances. She wore the epoch like a second skin, her attire blending the timeless elegance of her Moorish heritage with the daring cuts of contemporary fashion. Safwan matched her stride, his regal features set in a mask of determination, a silent testimony to centuries of survival against the relentless march of time.

The night beckoned them with its siren call, and they answered, drawn to the glittering epicenter of human revelry. They slipped into parties where chandeliers dripped diamonds and champagne flowed like rivers. Here, amidst the social elite, Aurya found herself a queen once more, her charm an invisible thread weaving through the crowd, pulling the strings of conversation and laughter.

Safwan watched her with a mix of admiration and sorrow, knowing the power she wielded was born of a darkness they both shared. He conversed with tycoons and starlets, his eloquence reminiscent of a prince addressing his court. Yet behind his gilded words, there lurked a shadow of the melancholy that had become his constant companion.

With every encounter, they spun their web, the unsuspecting guests none the wiser. Immortality afforded them the luxury of patience, and they played the long game, each smile a tactic, each gesture part of a grander strategy. The night was their domain, and within it, they moved with an assurance that only those unbound by the constraints of mortality could possess.

Amidst the swirl of music and laughter, Aurya felt her spirit soar, even as her soul remained tethered to the weight of eternity. And while Safwan mingled with feigned interest, his thoughts wandered to quieter places, to dreams of life cycles he could observe but never partake in.

In this city of dreams, they danced on the edge of a knife, their existence a paradox of endless time and ephemeral moments. But for now, they reveled in the masquerade, the dark prince and his enigmatic queen, hidden in plain sight among New York's glitterati, the pulse of the city echoing the undying rhythm of their hearts.

The night draped Manhattan in a velvet cloak, its skyscrapers like sentinels watching over the city's ceaseless rhythm. Aurya Alcazar sauntered through the throng with the grace of a feline predator, her dark eyes shimmering like pools of obsidian under the neon lights. The scent of stale cigarettes and perfumed bodies mingled in the air, a testament to humanity's pursuit of pleasure amidst the concrete jungle.

In a dimly lit lounge, she leaned against the mahogany bar, her presence commanding the room. Aurya's lips curled into a knowing smile as she caught the gaze of a silver-haired businessman nursing a scotch on the rocks. He was ensnared by her allure, a marionette awaiting its master's pull.

"Another round for my friend here," Aurya purred, gesturing toward the man with a flick of her wrist. Her voice, a siren's call, resonated with an ancient timbre that belied her youthful visage.

The businessman, intoxicated by Aurya's charm, nodded fervently, his inhibitions dissolving like sugar in hot tea. She drew closer, weaving words laced with promises and innuendos. Within moments, he divulged secrets better kept behind boardroom doors—trade routes, mergers, market predictions—all laid bare before her. Aurya listened, her mind cataloging each revelation, a spider meticulously tending to her web.

Meanwhile, Safwan Amin wandered the twilight streets, his silhouette a solitary figure against the backdrop of familial warmth glowing from restaurant windows. His gaze lingered on a young couple sharing a milkshake, two straws bridging the distance between them—a simple act of communion that he could never truly experience.

A pang of yearning twisted in his chest as he observed children chasing fireflies in Central Park. Their laughter pierced the serenity of the night, a stark reminder of the life cycles from which he was forever barred. Safwan sat on a secluded bench, his form obscured by the shadows of towering oaks. He watched, an eternal outsider, as families packed up their picnic baskets and folded their blankets, leaving nothing but footprints and echoes of joy in their wake.

The world moved around him, a carousel of lives spinning with the promise of new days, while he remained static, cursed with remembrance and a heart that beat out of time. Safwan sighed, the sound a whisper lost amidst the hum of the city, his loneliness a shroud that not even the vibrancy of 1960s New York City could penetrate.

In these parallel existences, Aurya and Safwan danced a dance of divergence, one reveling in the power of eternal youth, the other suffocating under the weight of immortal isolation. As the night waned, the city's pulse continued unabated, indifferent to the plight of two souls bound together yet drifting apart in the vastness of time and the labyrinth of human desires.

The city thrummed with the heartbeat of ambition, and Aurya Alcazar had her finger firmly on its pulse. Glamour became her armor and fashion her weapon, each creation a tapestry woven from the threads of timelessness. She draped fabric over mannequins like secrets whispered into the night, her designs bold declarations in the cacophony of New York's elite. Critics and admirers alike waited with bated breath as Aurya unveiled her latest collection, one that defied the constraints of mortality with its audacious lines and immortal elegance.

In the glow of arc lights and flashbulbs, she watched models strut down the runway, their forms swathed in garments that seemed to capture the very essence of the decades. There was power in the way the silk hugged their bodies, a silent testament to Aurya's cunning intellect and relentless drive for excellence. The audience, rapturous under her spell, could not fathom the centuries of artistry that pulsed beneath the surface of her enigmatic smile. She knew the fleeting nature of trends; how easily they ebbed and flowed like the tides of history she had witnessed. Yet, she remained the vanguard, her immortality granting her an uncanny foresight that kept her perpetually ahead of the curve.

While Aurya's star ascended in the firmament of high fashion, Safwan Amin walked the cold, unforgiving streets of Manhattan, his heart heavy with a longing no amount of success could sate. He treaded through neighborhoods where laughter echoed from brownstone stoops and love lingered in the sweet smoggy air. But these human joys were not for him to claim. The further Aurya drifted into her realm of opulence and acclaim, the more acutely he felt the chasm between them widen. His days teemed with restless exploration, each alleyway and avenue a potential breadcrumb trail leading to the end of their eternal night.

He poured over ancient texts and modern philosophies in dimly lit libraries, seeking a salve for their cursed existence. In the leather-bound tomes, he traced the words of those who had pondered the great mysteries before him, their musings now dust-laden echoes in the vaults of time. Yet, no answer yielded itself readily, leaving Safwan ensnared in a labyrinth of existential quandaries, his spirit fraying at the edges like the pages of the books he so desperately scoured.

Their paths, once so entwined, diverged like the branching lines of fate—a designer and a dreamer caught in a dance of disparity. Aurya reveled in the intoxicating allure of power, her name etched in the annals of a mortal world she would forever elude. Meanwhile, Safwan wandered through the pulsing cityscape, a ghost among the living, searching for a release that seemed as elusive as the grasp of dawn's first light upon the horizon.

Underneath the weight of centuries, the fabric of their union began to fray, pulled taut by the relentless pursuit of purpose and passion. And as the city that never sleeps continued its eternal march, Aurya and Safwan found themselves adrift in the currents of immortality, each seeking solace in the embrace of an ever-elusive peace.

The neon-lit skyline of New York City flickered like a tempestuous sea, reflecting the storm brewing in Aurya's dark eyes. Velvet night draped over Manhattan, its cover concealing the fractured fault lines running beneath the surface of an immortal relationship. The air swirled with the pungent aroma of ambition and the relentless energy of lives lived on a mortal coil—lives that Aurya and Safwan had outpaced by centuries yet found themselves ensnared within.

Aurya, once a noblewoman of al-Andalus, now flitted through the city's opulent underworld as a seductive siren. With each passing night, her transformation into the club queen solidified, her very aura infused with the hedonistic beat of the music that pulsed through the cavernous venues she prowled. Her laughter—a melodic chimera of delight and malice—echoed off the walls as she danced, her movements a mesmerizing spell cast upon all who watched.

Safwan, his regal demeanor shadowed by the weight of ennui, observed from the fringes, his presence a silent testament to their growing chasm. Where Aurya sought the fervor of adoration, he yearned for the simplicity of a single, unending heartbeat that could signal an end to this eternal waltz of nightfall.

Their battles erupted sporadically, fierce clashes of wills and wants that left their surroundings charged with electric resentment. Accusations were volleyed with the precision of archers, each word a piercing arrow aimed to wound deeply. Jealousy gnawed at them, a ravenous beast unleashed by their need for validation from transient souls they both knew would wither with time.

"Your thirst for these...mortals," Safwan's voice cut through the smoky haze of the latest soirée, "it eclipses us."

"Us?" Aurya's retort was a whip crack, her eyes flashing dangerously. "What 'us' is there to speak of, when you spend your nights courting shadows and dust?"

Their immortality, once a bond stronger than any forged steel, now felt like chains that tethered them to separate shores. And as Aurya delved deeper into her newfound power, her ability to manipulate desires and destinies, Safwan recoiled, his gaze turning ever inward to the void they could not fill.

The dance floor became Aurya's domain, each step a declaration of her indomitable spirit, each twirl an act of defiance against the passage of time. Men gravitated towards her like moths to a flame, eager to bask in the glow of her ephemeral attention, oblivious to the pyre they courted.

Safwan's silhouette lingered in doorways, his eyes tracing the contours of families sharing tender moments. His heart, still capable of so much love, contracted with the pain of knowing such connections eluded him, like whispers just beyond hearing.

"Who are we, Aurya?" he murmured one evening, his words barely rising above the cacophony of life around them. "What have we become in this endless night?"

She didn't answer, lost in the thrall of another round of applause, another suitor ensnared. Safwan turned away, his form dissolving into the crowd, his question lingering unanswered in the space between them. The divide grew wider, their paths diverging further, as New York City hummed with the oblivious rhythm of the living and the cursed dance of two immortals veered towards its inexorable end.

The velvet curtain fell with a hush, a whisper of silk parting to reveal Aurya Alcazar at the zenith of her earthly dominion.

Spotlights converged on her like celestial bodies orbiting a dark star, casting her raven hair and pallid skin in an ethereal glow. She stood, a monolith of fashion, her latest design cascading around her—a tapestry of midnight lace and shimmering jewels that clung to her form as if born from shadow itself.

The crowd erupted, a cacophony of adulation that filled the cavernous hall of the Manhattan gallery. Critics and moguls alike clamored for her attention, their praises laced with the intoxicating promise of fortune and renown. With each flutter of her eyelashes, deals were struck; with a mere tilt of her head, alliances formed. Aurya reveled in her power, the sway she held over this mortal coil, yet each triumph etched a deeper chasm between her and the prince who once shared her heart.

In the quiet recesses of an aged library, far removed from the opulence of the runway, Safwan Amin wrestled with the weight of eternity. His fingers traced the weathered spines of ancient texts and modern tomes, their pages brimming with musings on life, death, and the esoteric spaces between. The scent of musty leather was a pungent reminder of the countless lives that flickered and faded while he remained, an observer locked outside the realm of time.

"Is there no respite?" he whispered to the silent stacks, his voice a mere ghost of sound amidst the stillness. "No end to this relentless march?" He sought solace in the words of philosophers long gone, their discourse on morality and existence a balm to his weary soul. Yet, where they spoke of finality, he found only the echo of his own unending tale.

As night descended upon the city, its smelly, bustling streets alive with the pulse of human endeavor, Safwan emerged from his refuge. The glare of neon signs cast harsh shadows across his features, sculpting his noble visage into something otherworldly, haunted. A profound loneliness clutched at him, a specter more chilling than any horror he had faced in his centuries of wandering.

He watched from afar as Aurya's image graced the cover of every magazine, her name a siren's call that beckoned the elite from their havens of excess. Her success—a blazing comet streaking across the sky—felt distant, foreign, as if she inhabited a world beyond his reach. The bond that had once tethered them through the maelstrom of history now strained, threatening to snap under the pressure of her ascent.

Aurya, meanwhile, stood alone in the glare of the after-party, the air sweet with the cloying scent of champagne and victory. Applause still rang in her ears, a hollow symphony that failed to stir her cold heart. She gazed into the throng of admirers, searching for the familiar light brown eyes that had always anchored her. But Safwan was absent, his absence a void more profound than the silence that followed the storm of cheers.

In the solitude of her triumph, Aurya felt the immortality they both cursed wrap around her like a shroud, suffocating the very fires of ambition that had driven her to such dizzying heights. Power, once an intoxicating elixir, now tasted bitter on her tongue. She yearned for the simplicity of a mortal life—a fleeting moment of true connection—but fate had spun a different tale for her, a tale woven with threads of darkness and eternity.

And so, beneath the glimmering facade of success, Aurya Alcazar, the undying fashion icon, stood more isolated than ever. The ghosts of her past whispered of love and sacrifice, but the future loomed, an abyss from which no light escaped. Safwan, her eternal consort, turned his gaze toward the heavens, seeking answers in the stars that had borne witness to their sorrowful odyssey—an immortal searching for the end of forever.

The velvet night clung to the walls of their penthouse, a dark tapestry against the shimmering city lights of Manhattan. Aurya stood by the towering windows, her silhouette ethereal, framed by the opulent drapery that whispered secrets of grandeur and isolation. Below, the city throbbed with life, indifferent to the turmoil brewing in the cold expanse above.

"Your shows... they eclipse even the stars," Safwan's voice cut through the quiet, its timbre strained like the strings of an ancient lute.

Aurya turned, her eyes reflecting the gleam of a skyline that knew no sleep, no surrender. "And what of it, Safwan? Shall I dim my light to match the darkness you've cloaked yourself in?" Her words, sharp as shards of broken crystal, betrayed the chasm yawning between them.

"Is this our fate then?" he asked, the pain evident beneath his composed facade. "To be lost in the labyrinth of your making, where the Minotaur is your ambition, insatiable and monstrous?"

"Speak not of monsters," she retorted, her gaze piercing him like a lance. "For we both share the curse that makes us kin to such creatures."

Their exchange crackled with the electricity of a tempest, charged with the weight of centuries and the sorrow of two souls bound in an endless dance. The air grew heavy, laden with unspoken regrets and the scent of jasmine that seemed to mock their plight.

"Once, we sought the shadows together," Safwan murmured, his voice a lamentation. "Now, the limelight blinds you, Aurya, and I wander alone in the penumbra of your triumphs."

"Would you have me forsake this world that adores me?" Her laughter was hollow, echoing off the marble and glass like the tolling of a bell. "For a love that withers in the glare of my success?"

"Love should not wither," he said solemnly. "It should be the one constant in our turbulent eternity."

"Constants are illusions, princely one." Aurya's voice quivered with the onset of despair. "Illusions as fragile as the mortals who birth them."

Their argument spiraled into silence, a void punctuated only by the distant hum of the city that never sleeps. Aurya sank into the depths of an antique chair, her body feeling the burden of years that no time could erode. She closed her eyes, seeking solace in the darkness behind her lids.

Safwan watched her, his chest tight with a grief that had no name. He realized then that the woman before him, cloaked in success and adulation, was but a phantom of the Aurya he had loved—a wraith draped in the trappings of power that promised everything yet gave nothing.

He longed to reach out to her, to bridge the chasm of their own creation, but the words died on his lips. What solace could he offer when he himself was adrift in the same sea of desolation?

Aurya opened her eyes, and for a moment, the glittering cityscape held no allure. The void within her yawned wider, a maw threatening to consume the last vestiges of her humanity. She had yearned for immortality, for a place among the stars, but now she found herself suffocating under the weight of an eternal crown.

"Perhaps," she whispered, her voice barely audible over the cacophony of the city below, "our greatest folly was believing we could defy the laws of nature without consequence."

"Perhaps," Safwan replied, his heart heavy with resignation. "But even gods can fall, Aurya. Even gods can feel the sting of their own hubris."

In that solemn chamber, high above the world of fleeting lives and ephemeral dreams, two immortals grappled with the paradox of their existence. Power had been their wish, but at what cost? The answer lay hidden in the shadows of their own making, a truth too painful to confront.

And so, amidst the splendor of their gilded cage, Aurya and Safwan stood on the precipice of an uncertain future, each haunted by the specter of a love that struggled to survive in the face of an undying world.

The night air in Manhattan was thick with the scent of rain-soiled asphalt, a stark contrast to the sterile opulence Aurya had wrapped around herself like a shroud. She watched from her penthouse balcony as Safwan disappeared into the thrumming heart of the city, his form swallowed by the faceless crowd below.

In the distance, Times Square dazzled—a cacophony of neon and noise, an illusion of vibrancy that mirrored Aurya's own facade of invincibility. But tonight, the city's pulse beat out of sync with her own. A chill whispered across her skin, an omen of the solitude encroaching upon her soul.

Safwan's footsteps echoed a grim rhythm as he navigated the labyrinthine streets, each step drawing him further away from the empire of sorrow they had built together. The flickering streetlamps cast elongated shadows that danced around him, mocking specters of the life he could never lead, a life where time's relentless march brought change, growth, decay—anything but this perpetual limbo.

Nestled within the modest walls of a quaint apartment, Melanie Preacher hummed softly to herself, lost in the simple contentment of grading papers by the warm glow of a table lamp. Melanie's world was small, comforting in its boundaries, a stark contrast to the endless horizon of eternity that Safwan now traversed. Her laughter, bright and untainted, spilled into the room like sunlight breaking through storm clouds. It was a sound Safwan found he hungered for, more than blood, more than power, more than anything the immortal coil could offer.

Aurya's fingers curled into fists at her sides as she envisioned Safwan seeking solace in that tender sanctuary. For centuries, their love had been a fortress, impregnable and unyielding, but now, it seemed as fragile as the silken threads of a spider's web, glistening with the dew of treachery and poised to snap under the weight of unspoken desires.

Driven by a tempest of jealousy and fear, Aurya descended into the city's abyss, her heels clicking a staccato warning on the stone. She would not allow the chasm between them to widen. She would not be usurped by the innocence of a mortal woman, no matter how sweet her song.

Safwan paused outside Melanie's door, the wood grain rough beneath his fingertips. To knock was to invite hope—a dangerous thing for a man cursed with the burden of eternity. Yet, there remained within him a spark, a defiant ember that refused to be extinguished, fed by the possibility of a connection unmarred by the rot of immortality.

Within the confines of Melanie's home, the world narrowed to the space between two heartbeats—the teacher's, so full of vibrant life; the prince's, a haunted echo of what once was. There, amidst the mundane trappings of domesticity, Safwan allowed himself to believe in the illusion of normalcy, even as it slipped through his grasp like grains of sand.

Aurya arrived unseen, a wraith veiled in the shadows of the city's underbelly. Her eyes, twin pools of ancient darkness, fixed on the apartment with a predator's focus. Whatever it took, she would reclaim what was hers. Her love for Safwan was a tempest, fierce and all-consuming, and she would weather the storm of his betrayal, bend him back to her will.

With the silence of a confession and the gravity of a verdict, Aurya made her way toward the quiet refuge that held the heart she sought to possess. The night held its breath, and the city watched, a silent witness to the unfolding tragedy. In the pursuit of immortality, they had forsaken the very essence of life, and now, as Aurya plotted her course through the tangled skein of love and obsession, the price of that folly loomed ever larger.

For in the end, what is eternity without the one who gives it meaning?

The first snowflakes of the season drifted past the fogged window, settling like silent witnesses upon the world outside Melanie's apartment. Inside, the air was thick with the musk of human desire, a scent that Safwan had learned to mimic but never truly felt—until now.

The softness of Melanie's skin beneath his fingertips stirred an unfamiliar yearning within him—an ache for something genuine and untainted by the curse of eternity. Her breathless moans echoed in the dimly lit room, a sweet symphony that pulled at his soul with a longing he could scarcely understand.

But as passion gave way to the primal hunger that lurked in the marrow of his ancient bones, Safwan's control slipped. The taste of blood—rich and intoxicating—flooded his senses. It took just a moment, a heartbeat's lapse, for the man to recede and the monster within to claim its due.

With each draught, the light in Melanie's deep green eyes dimmed, her life force ebbing into the chasm of his unending thirst. When the last flicker of her spirit extinguished, Safwan came crashing back to the harrowing truth. He had devoured her innocence, destroyed the naïve beauty that had drawn him to her side.

A guttural cry tore from his throat—a sound not heard for centuries—as he cradled the fragile shell of what had been Melanie Preacher. The snow outside no longer seemed pure, but accusatory, a cold blanket covering the sins of the night.

He stumbled from the warmth of the room into the cruel embrace of winter, leaving behind the remnants of a dream that had turned to ash in his mouth. The city's ceaseless pulse mocked his solitude, its bright lights a garish contrast to the darkness that enveloped his heart.

When Safwan found Aurya, she was perched on the edge of the world they had once vowed to conquer together, her raven hair a stark silhouette against the city's glow. She turned to him, her expression a tapestry woven with threads of concern and sovereignty.

"Something has broken," he whispered, the weight of his actions bowing him lower than any crown ever had.

Aurya drew him close, her arms encircling him in an embrace that spoke of battles fought and storms weathered. Yet there was a tremor in her touch, the slight hesitation that betrayed her fear of losing him.

"Tell me," she urged, her voice a beacon in the tempest of his despair.

Safwan recounted the night's horror, each word a stone cast into the still waters of their existence, rippling outward with the inevitability of consequence. As he spoke of Melanie's death—her blood on his lips, her light extinguished by his hand—the gravity of their immortal plight pressed down upon them both.

"Then we are truly damned," he murmured, the finality of it searing his tongue.

"Perhaps," Aurya conceded, her dark eyes searching his face for solace neither could provide. "Or perhaps this is our awakening."

"An awakening," Safwan echoed hollowly. "Or the beginning of the end."

"Both require a choice," she said softly, the wisdom of centuries lining her words.

In the silence that followed, Safwan knew that the path he must walk was one of penance and solitude, a journey that Aurya, for all her love and power, could not share. With a resolve born of grief and love, he uttered the words that would unbind their fates.

"Then let us choose... to go separate ways."

Snowflakes, each a silent witness to the centuries-old tragedy unfolding below, drifted through the frigid New York air. Aurya and Safwan, two immortals bound by love and curse, stood amidst the waning glow of a streetlamp, its light flickering like the final beats of a dying heart.

Safwan's voice was firm, yet it carried an undercurrent of desolation that cut through the winter chill. The words hung between them, a death knell tolling for their shared eternity.

Aurya's gaze lingered on him, her dark eyes pools of midnight reflecting the storm within. She was beauty and sorrow intertwined, a tempest cloaked in the guise of a woman. "To sever what fate has entwined is no trifling matter," she whispered, her tone laced with the wisdom of ages and the weariness of a soul stretched thin across time.

"Perhaps," Safwan replied, his regal stance belying the tremble of emotion that threatened to shatter his composure. "But to continue together is to deny ourselves the chance at peace—whatever semblance of it we can grasp."

The silence that followed was punctuated only by the distant sounds of the city—a city oblivious to the epochal shift occurring within its shadows. They were statues carved from the very essence of night, motionless as the world moved around them.

"Will you return to the fashion that has embraced you?" Safwan asked, the question holding more than a hint of resignation. His eyes traced the outline of her face, memorizing the contours as if they were precious script in an ancient tome.

"Perhaps," Aurya echoed, her voice now distant, a zephyr carrying the scent of bygone eras. "Or perhaps I will find a new canvas upon which to cast my shadow."

"And I," Safwan breathed out, "must seek the solace of oblivion, away from the specter of death that clings to my being." It was a confession, an admission of his deepest longing—to be free from the endless night that cradled them both.

"Oblivion," Aurya mused, her lips parting in a smile that did not reach her eyes. "A lover far crueler than I."

"Yet one that offers an end," he countered, the weight of unshed tears gleaming like jewels in his eyes.

Aurya reached out, her fingers brushing against the cold fabric of his coat—once, twice—before drawing back. "Then we part, my prince, as all stars are destined to drift apart in the vastness of the heavens."

"Until the cosmos brings us together once more," Safwan added, his voice breaking on the edge of hope and despair.

"Until then," Aurya affirmed.

With a final look that spoke volumes of love and regret, they turned from each other, their silhouettes receding into the embrace of the city's labyrinthine streets. Two immortal souls, each embarking on solitary paths carved by choice and circumstance, leaving behind the remnants of a bond that had defied time itself.

As they disappeared into the night—Safwan towards the quiet refuge of darkened alleys, Aurya towards the glittering allure of Manhattan's skyline—the snow continued to fall, erasing their footsteps, as if the world sought to forget the existence of those who could never belong to it.

Chapter 5

صدع "Rift"

Aurya Alcazar reclined on the velvet chaise of her penthouse, a monument to wealth high above the city's incessant heartbeat. Sunlight filtered through the floor-to-ceiling windows, casting prisms over the cold marble and gilded edges that framed her world. Yet, no amount of opulence could fill the void; her eyes, those deep wells of eternal sorrow, skimmed with disinterest over the numbers and figures that sprawled across the bank statements in her hands.

Her lips, once full of fervent prayers whispered in the moonlit gardens of al-Andalus, now curved into a frown. A sigh escaped her—a whisper lost amid the rustling of paper—the sound of boredom and frustration intermingling like the perfumed guests at a ball she had no desire to attend. The tactile sensation of wealth did little to sate her hunger, a hunger far more profound than the emptiness of her coffers.

As dusk approached, painting the skyline with shades of regret and longing, Aurya prepared for the evening's hunt. With practiced ease, she slipped into the persona of the enchantress, draping her lithe form in fabrics that whispered against her skin, as ethereal as her pallid complexion. Her raven hair cascaded down her back, a river of darkness that promised depths untold.

In the heart of the city, amidst towering monuments to man's ceaseless ambition, Aurya found her quarry—a wealthy businessman, ripe with the arrogance of self-made success. The air around them grew thick with her seductive charm, invisible threads weaving a web from which he could not hope to escape. She touched his arm lightly, and the gesture alone was enough to tilt the axis of his world, bending him to her indomitable will.

"Your generosity knows no bounds," she murmured, her voice a melody that danced upon the edge of temptation. Each word was a calculated step in the intricate dance of predation.

The man, caught in her gaze, nodded eagerly as he signed away a fortune without a second thought. The pen in his hand moved with a life of its own, choreographed by Aurya's unseen influence. As their fingers brushed, she allowed herself to feel a momentary pulse of his life essence—warm, vibrant, unsuspecting.

With a veil of cold detachment descending upon her features, Aurya drew upon the dark gift bestowed upon her centuries ago. The act was familiar, yet it never ceased to chill her to the bone. She watched the vitality drain from him, his robust frame slumping, his eyes clouding over with weakness and vulnerability. He was but a husk now, a discarded shell left adrift in the wake of her unrelenting need.

As the man staggered away, his steps uncertain and heavy with sudden fatigue, Aurya turned her back to him, her silhouette a stark contrast against the city's electric glow. She felt neither triumph nor guilt, only an acute awareness of the curse that bound her—immortality, a double-edged sword that cut deeper with each passing century.

She pondered the ancient symbols and cryptic messages that haunted her dreams, the whispers of past and future that coiled around her fate like serpents. In the solitude of her penthouse, surrounded by the silent witnesses of her undying existence, Aurya Alcazar stood alone—a queen in a kingdom of shadows, her reign as endless as the stars that watched over her.

Safwan's silhouette moved like a shadow through the cacophonous tapestry of Marrakech's marketplace, where colors danced and exotic scents played upon the air. The sun cast a golden hue over stalls laden with spices and silks, their vibrant oranges and reds competing with the sheer intensity of life teeming around him. But his eyes, those deep wells of hope and ancient sorrow, were fixed on a prize beyond the material allure of this place.

"Tell me your secrets," he would murmur, leaning close to the wizened faces of local scholars and mystics who guarded their knowledge like precious jewels. His voice was tinged with the persuasive lilt of royalty, even as it bore the weight of centuries. With each conversation, he wove his way closer to the truth about their undying curse, his heart beating a determined rhythm against the cage of immortality that bound him.

Meanwhile, across the sea, in a Parisian palace where decadence reigned supreme, Aurya made her entrance. The grand ballroom swirled with the excess of the age, laughter tinkling like crystal amid the rustle of silk and the clink of fine china. Socialites draped in jewels and artists lost in their lofty ideals spun around her, blissfully unaware of the predator in their midst.

Aurya floated through the crowd, her movements a choreographed ballet perfected over lifetimes. She engaged in conversations that skimmed the surface like stones over still water, her replies measured and honeyed. Yet beneath the facade, her ennui was a gaping chasm, threatening to swallow her whole. Her gaze cut through the masquerade of mirth, seeking out those whose life force called to her parched soul, a siren's song of sustenance and damnation entwined.

The night unfurled around her, a dark tapestry upon which she painted with strokes of longing and fleeting pleasure. Yet, even as she partook of the revelry, her thoughts drifted to

Safwan, the prince of her heart and fellow captive of eternity. Their dance was one of fire and ice, desire and despair—a pas de deux as timeless as the stars that blanketed the night sky outside the glittering windows of the palatial estate.

Safwan's fingers traced the contours of ancient leather, his touch reverent as he eased open the cover of a tome that whispered secrets from its dusty pages. The library of Cairo, a sanctuary of forgotten wisdom, enveloped him within its venerable embrace, the musty air thick with the scent of parchments long undisturbed. Shafts of sunlight pierced the dimness, casting golden beams that danced upon the texts like silent guardians of history.

The shelves bowed under the weight of centuries, lined with scrolls and manuscripts whose faded ink told tales of civilizations risen and fallen. Safwan's gaze was unyielding, his purpose singular as he scoured each line for any whisper of their curse. Beneath the furrow of his brow, his eyes glowed with an ember of determination, the same flame that had burned through the ages, refusing to be extinguished.

In the hushed stillness, only the soft rustle of paper could be heard as he turned pages with meticulous care, his mind piecing together fragments of lore—a hieroglyph here, a cryptic verse there—each a tantalizing glimpse into the enigma that bound him and Aurya to an eternity neither desired.

***

Meanwhile, in Milan, the pulse of modernity beat in stark contrast to Cairo's timeless rhythm. Aurya found herself amidst the splendor of a fashion show, the runway alight with the latest visions of couture. The room thrummed with anticipation, cameras ready to capture the spectacle of creativity unleashed.

Vivid hues sashayed down the catwalk, draping the models in swathes of fabric that defied convention and teased the senses.

Avant-garde designs blossomed in an array of textures and patterns, a testament to the fearless spirit of human artistry. For a fleeting moment, Aurya allowed herself to be captivated, her immortal heart beating in sync with the collective awe that filled the air.

She navigated the sea of high society with an elegance born of her noble lineage, her smile a practiced curve that hinted at pleasures untold. Yet behind the facade, her soul languished in solitude, the emptiness echoing in the caverns where mortal joy once resided. Her laughter mingled with the elite, a melodic veneer that cloaked the void within, even as her eyes remained vigilant, ever searching for a connection that might transcend the bounds of time.

In the glittering lights and shadowed corners of the world, two souls wandered—one among ancient relics, the other in the embrace of transient beauty—each seeking solace from the relentless march of immortality.

Safwan's breath came in visible puffs, each one a misty ghost vanishing into the frigid air of the hidden cave. The Himalayan terrain was merciless—a jagged tapestry of ice and stone that had claimed many lives. Yet here he stood, unyielded, at the mouth of an abyss that promised answers or oblivion. His leather boots crunched against the snow, the sound a crisp betrayal of silence in the hallowed expanse.

The icy wind clawed through his heavy cloak, but his resolve burned hotter with every step he took into the cavern's gaping maw. Shadows clung to the walls like dark sentinels, their whispers ancient and untouched by time. Safwan's path was lit only by the flickering dance of the torch he held, its flame battling the oppressive darkness ahead.

Each step echoed a prayer for guidance, his heart a steady drumbeat against the encroaching stillness. Here, in this sanctum of solitude, he could feel the weight of centuries upon his shoulders, the burden of immortality that bound him to Aurya—a bond wrought by love, sealed by darkness. The promise of release shimmered on the edge of his consciousness, a distant star in the night of his existence.

Eyes keen and senses honed by countless nights, Safwan navigated the treacherous paths that spiraled ever downward. Stalactites hung from the ceiling like frozen spears, nature's silent guardians challenging his advance. He slipped once, twice, his hands scraping against the unforgiving rock, but his spirit never faltered. For Safwan knew that within these cold depths dwelled a sage whose wisdom might hold the key to their salvation—or condemn them to eternity.

Meanwhile, the pulse of Berlin's underground club scene throbbed like a living entity, its heartbeat resonating through the dimly lit enclave where Aurya found herself engulfed by a sea of writhing bodies. The music was a relentless surge, waves of bass rolling over the crowd in rhythmic domination. Strobe lights cut through the darkness, illuminating faces caught in moments of abandon—none more so than Aurya's.

Amidst the chaos, she danced. There was something primal about her movements, each sway and turn an invocation of her predatory grace—a fluidity born not of the music but of the night itself. Her raven hair whipped around her pale visage, strands catching the stuttering light as if weaving spells to enthrall those who dared look upon her.

In this cavernous underworld, Aurya was both sovereign and specter, her presence commanding yet ethereal. She moved among the revelers, a phantom bathed in neon glow, her skin a stark contrast against the dark allure of her attire. To the mortals around her, she was an enigma, a creature of beauty shrouded in the mystique of the unknown.

Yet, even as she surrendered to the rhythm, letting the beats consume her senses, there was no forgetting the void that gnawed at her soul. Immortality was her cruel consort, and it exacted its price with each ephemeral connection she made. The revelry was but a temporary salve, a fleeting reprieve from the endless march of days and nights that stretched before her like an infinite road to nowhere.

And so she danced—her body a vessel of yearning, her heart a chalice of longing—with the shadows whispering of a love lost to time and a life that yearned for the dawn of mortality.

Beneath the whispering canopy of cherry blossoms, Safwan's footsteps were silent, yet his presence resounded through the Zen garden's immaculate symmetry. Kyoto's ancient monastery stood as an oasis of peace amidst a world that knew little rest, its stones and streams a testament to the enduring search for enlightenment. The air was perfumed with incense, weaving a spell of tranquility that even time seemed to honor with hushed reverence.

He approached the monks, their saffron robes a stark flame against the soft greens and muted browns of their surroundings. With each step closer, the weight of centuries pressed upon him, a reminder of his endless pilgrimage through the corridors of eternity. His eyes, brimming with the wisdom of countless dawns and dusks, met theirs in silent greeting—a fraternity transcending the spoken word.

"Desire is the root of suffering," voiced an elder monk, his gaze piercing the veil of Safwan's soul.

"Yet to desire an end to desire—is this not also a form of longing?" Safwan replied, his voice a low thrum of weariness and hope entwined.

The monk's lips curved in a knowing smile, the exchange as much a dance of intellects as it was a duel. Here, in the heart of serenity, Safwan grappled with enigmas that promised no simple release; each answer found only birthed more questions, a Sisyphean struggle against the boulder of immortality.

Across the seas, where the Aegean caressed the Grecian shores with frothy fingers, Aurya surrendered to a different kind of embrace. The secluded villa, bathed in the glow of the Mediterranean sun, played host to her hedonistic retreat, a palace where pleasure and pain wore the same mask. Laughter mingled with the murmurs of the sea, a symphony of yearning that echoed within her hollowed heart.

She moved among her companions, a pantheon of Adonises and Aphrodites, each touch an electric current that coursed through her veins. Yet the electricity was fleeting, sparks against the cold expanse of her eternal solitude. Her every kiss was a paradox—both a feast and a famine—as she sought to sate the hunger that gnawed at the edges of her being.

"Are we not all prisoners of our own desires?" she whispered into the ear of a lover, her words carried away by the salt-kissed breeze.

In those moments of fervent connection, Aurya could almost forget the emptiness that awaited her when dawn's first light breached the horizon. Her body moved with a grace born of timeless beauty, but her spirit remained shackled to the shadows of what once was and what might never be again.

As the moon ascended to its throne in the night sky, both prince and noblewoman found themselves adrift in their respective solitudes. Safwan, amidst the stillness of the monastery garden, contemplated the cycle of life and death that he had transcended yet remained bound to. Aurya, gazing out at the endless expanse of the ocean, felt the relentless pull of the tides that mirrored the ebb and flow of her own immortal curse.

Two souls, united by a love that defied the ages, now faced the twilight of their existence apart—each seeking salvation in a world that offered them nothing but the illusion of peace and the certainty of longing.

Safwan stepped lightly into the embrace of the Amazon, the dense canopy a verdant vault above him. The air hummed with life—every chirp and rustle a testament to the forest's untamed heart. Splashes of color darted between the trees as parrots took flight, their plumage a vibrant contrast against the greenery. The scent of damp earth mingled with the sweet tang of exotic fruits, assaulting his senses as he ventured deeper into the wilderness.

He was a stranger here, yet the tribes welcomed him, recognizing a fellow soul marred by time's relentless march. They spoke little, communicating instead through gestures and the shared language of ritual. With painted faces and feathered adornments, they ushered him into their midst, inviting him to partake in ceremonies as ancient as the land itself. The beat of drums pulsed like the heartbeat of the earth, reverberating through Safwan's chest as he moved to their rhythm, his body surrendering to the sacred dance.

As dusk fell, the embers of a great fire cast flickering shadows on the participants' faces. Safwan's gaze was drawn into the flame, where the dance of orange and red seemed to whisper of secrets long forgotten. Here, amidst the ancestral spirits and the wisdom of shamans, Safwan sought an understanding that eluded him—a path towards redemption or perhaps the finality of peace.

Miles away, Aurya stood alone in her opulent penthouse in Dubai—a palace suspended in the heavens. She approached the floor-to-ceiling windows, her reflection a ghostly specter against the backdrop of a city alight with a thousand fires. Below her, the undulating dunes met the skyline, blurring the lines between nature and mankind's audacious monuments.

The penthouse was a silent cathedral of luxury, each piece of furniture curated to reflect wealth and taste. Yet, the sumptuous silks and cold marbles did little to warm the chill that had settled deep within her bones. She turned from the view, her movements deliberate, the weight of eternity pressing down upon her shoulders.

In the quietude of her sanctuary, Aurya allowed herself a moment of vulnerability. Her eyes, usually so full of cunning and resolve, now mirrored the skyscrapers' hollow glow. Longing etched into the fine lines at their corners, while resignation drew her elegant brows together. She yearned for something more—more than this endless game of power, more than the transient pleasures that had long since lost their luster.

"Is this all there is?" she murmured, her voice barely rising above the whisper of the night wind. Her question hung unanswered in the opulence of her isolation, an echo of a torment as old as time itself.

Together and apart, the prince and the noblewoman traversed their separate paths—a journey without end, two immortals bound to the world and yet beyond its reach. Their search for release, for a semblance of meaning in the face of eternal life, continued to unfold beneath the indifferent stars.

Safwan's fingers traced the ancient symbols etched into the cold stone walls of the hidden cave, the dim light from his torch casting flickering shadows that danced like specters in the hallowed space. The air was thick with the scent of moss and earth, a testament to the age of the place, where whispers of bygone eras seemed to reverberate with every heartbeat. Here, beneath the timeless Scottish Highlands, he was a solitary figure amidst relics of a forgotten past, each artifact a silent sentinel to his ceaseless quest.

The prince's brow furrowed as he examined a particularly cryptic inscription. It spoke of powers beyond mortal ken—a secret that could perhaps unlock the shackle of their eternity. With meticulous care, he translated the archaic script, his pulse quickening with a blend of hope and unease. The chamber seemed to contract around him, the air growing heavier, as if charged with the weight of impending revelation.

A hidden mechanism yielded under his touch, and a portion of the wall receded with a rumble that echoed through the cavernous depths. Safwan's breath caught in his throat. Before him lay a chamber untouched by time, its contents veiled in shadows that even the bravest souls would fear to tread. He stood on the threshold, anticipation warring with dread. What power—or peril—might lie within?

Meanwhile, across the continent, Aurya Alcazar moved through the opulent halls of a Venetian palazzo, her presence a vision of ethereal grace amid the decadence of the masquerade ball. The air was alive with the sound of orchestral strings, the laughter of masked revelers, and the rich perfume of blooming flowers that adorned the grandiose space. Beneath the artful frescoes and crystal chandeliers, she was both a part of the spectacle and apart from it, her loneliness shrouded by the vibrancy of the festivity.

She accepted the hand of a stranger, allowing herself to be led in a dance that was both an escape and a reminder of the void within. Their movements were fluid, a harmony of two beings lost in the rhythm of an age-old melody. Her laughter rose above the music, a melodic counterpoint that concealed the sorrow etched upon her soul. Around her swirled a cavalcade of faces, none of which could see the aching emptiness behind her own exquisite mask.

As they spun, the hem of her gown whispered secrets across the marble floor, tales of love and loss that only the stones would remember. There, beneath the guise of merriment, Aurya was a phantom among phantoms, her immortal yearning as invisible to the crowd as the true faces hidden by their ornate disguises. Yet, even in the midst of such splendor, the ache for something more—a connection that transcended time itself—remained as persistent as the tides lapping at the city's ancient foundations.

The air in the remote temple was a sacred hush, thick with the scent of burning incense that spiraled toward the heavens in ethereal wisps. Safwan sat cross-legged on the cold stone floor, his hands resting lightly upon his knees, palms turned skyward in silent supplication. The fluttering of prayer flags outside whispered secrets to the mountain winds, while within, the only sound was the soft patter of dust motes dancing in the slants of light piercing the shadowed sanctuary.

Hours had passed—or had it been moments? Time held no dominion here. Safwan's mind, a fortress of focus, warded off the creeping tendrils of fatigue. His eyes, closed to the physical realm, beheld visions of ancient texts unfurling like petals, each word a beacon guiding him through the labyrinth of his immortality. He sought enlightenment, a path to release not just from this undying existence but also from the chains of guilt and longing that bound his spirit tighter than any curse.

Yet as the day waned and the chill of evening crept through the temple walls, Safwan's inner eye glimpsed a truth more haunting than any specter of the night: enlightenment promised peace, but could it fill the void left by centuries of solitude?

In a penthouse far removed from the Tibetan stillness, Aurya Alcazar stood alone amidst opulence that seemed to mock her emptiness. The panoramic vista of Dubai's glittering skyline stretched before her, a tapestry of light against the velvet darkness. She leaned against the cool glass, her reflection a ghostly echo of the woman who had once danced under the starlit skies of al-Andalus, whose heart had thrummed with hope and love.

Now, her heart was still as the marble beneath her bare feet, and the city's pulse—a symphony of life—could not stir the desolation that settled in her chest. She gazed out at the world, its myriad lives flickering and flaring in the distance, and felt an ache for something elusive, a connection that transcended the eons, that bridged the chasm between what she was and what she yearned to be.

Separated by vast lands and the weight of their shared history, Aurya and Safwan were united in their isolation. In the echoes of silence that surrounded them both, there was a resonance, a frequency that hummed with the sorrow of two souls intertwined by fate yet divided by their search for salvation. They longed not for the immortality that was their prison, but for the mortality that had slipped through their fingers like grains of sand lost to an endless desert.

As the moon ascended to its throne above the world, casting a silver glow over all it surveyed, Aurya turned from the window, the silk of her gown whispering across the floor like a lament. Safwan rose from his meditation, the shadows clinging to him as if reluctant to let go. The night held them in its embrace, a cocoon woven from the threads of their eternal journey—a journey that promised no end, only the faint hope of a destination that might one day grant them peace.

Chapter 6

النعيم "Bliss"

The grand hall of their mansion, nestled within the lush Portuguese landscape, shuddered with the resonance of their discord. Aurya Alcazar, her raven hair cascading over her shoulders like a dark waterfall, stood defiant before Prince Safwan, her posture rigid with centuries-old pride. The echoes of their raised voices collided with the ornate walls, each marbled pattern and gilded cornice absorbing the biting timbre of betrayal.

"Decades," she spat out, the word slicing through the lingering tension like a dagger's edge. "Decades, Safwan, and not even the shadow of your presence graced my solitude." Her chest heaved, the rise and fall betraying the storm of emotions swirling inside her immortal heart.

Safwan's gaze held hers, his eyes—the color of tumultuous seas—brimming with a sorrow that belied his regal stature. He opened his mouth to speak but found himself ensnared in the web of her bitterness.

"Imagine it, if your mind can stretch so far," Aurya continued, her voice a crescendo of anguish, "the dread of an eternity unfurling before you, barren of the only soul who ever understood the abyss within." A tangible coldness seeped from her words, frosting the air between them.

"Death itself became a siren's call I could not answer." She turned from him, her silhouette framed by the moonlight spilling in through the towering windows. "To be suspended in this forsaken state, where the sweet release of oblivion is forever just beyond reach—it is a cruelty you bestowed upon me."

Her vulnerability surfaced like a specter from the depths, haunting the silence that followed. The shadows seemed to lean closer, as if eager to witness the unfolding drama of two beings bound by an undying flame, yet scorched by its relentless burn.

"Would that I could have perished beneath the sun's searing kiss or lain to rest in a silvered tomb," she murmured, the softness of her tone belying the severity of her words. "But no death will claim me—no peace shall be mine. This is our everlasting legacy."

Aurya's fingers trailed along the velvet drapery, each touch a testament to the countless years that slipped through her grasp like grains of sand in an endless hourglass. There, amidst the splendor of a mansion that was both sanctuary and prison, the weight of her loneliness bore down upon her like the crush of the ocean's depths.

And in that moment, under the watchful eyes of painted ancestors and carved deities, they were nothing more than two souls ensnared in a dance as ancient and as tortured as time itself.

The grandeur of their quarrel lingered in the air long after Aurya's departure, its echoes dying like the last gasps of day succumbing to the onset of twilight. Safwan stood motionless, a silent statue amidst the opulence that mocked his internal disquiet. His heart, if such an undying organ could still be called that, hammered against the cage of his immortal flesh, each beat reverberating with the acute awareness of what had just transpired.

He closed his eyes, summoning the centuries of wisdom that immortality afforded him. The night outside beckoned, offering both concealment and revelation, a canvas upon which their story continued to unfold in strokes of pain and longing. With a deep breath that did not ease the tightness in his chest, he stepped through the threshold of the mansion, into the cool embrace of the Portuguese night.

Moonlight caressed the ancient stones of the labyrinth, a spectral touch that seemed to guide Aurya's steps even as she wandered, lost within her own mind as much as the hedges. Her gown whispered against the foliage, a sibilant secret shared only with the night. Here, in this twisted confluence of paths, she found a perverse reflection of her existence—endless choices leading ever back upon themselves, a journey without destination.

Aurya paused, the ghostly light casting her shadow onto the hedge wall. It stretched and contorted, a dark mimicry of her eternal state. She wondered if the garden felt the sting of her loneliness, if the roses wept with dew or merely with the night's chill. Around her, the silence was profound, broken only by the distant call of the sea, a reminder of the world's ceaseless turning—a world that moved on while she remained static, a prisoner of unforgiving time.

Within the confines of the labyrinth, thoughts swirled like the mist that began to rise from the earth, tendrils curling around her ankles as if seeking to anchor her to the spot. She contemplated the dual-edged sword of their love, a bond that had granted them eternity yet robbed them of the solace found in mortality's finality. She pondered the paradox of wanting to escape that which she could not bear to lose.

Safwan, emerging from the archway that led into the garden, felt the oppressive weight of the night's silence. The scent of jasmine hung heavy, a cloying perfume that could not mask the underlying decay of fallen petals beneath his feet. He knew the labyrinth well, each turn and dead end etched into his memory across the ages. Yet tonight, it seemed unfamiliar, as if reshaped by Aurya's turmoil.

He advanced, a solitary figure against the backdrop of nature's artful confusion. His voice, when he finally dared to break the quietude, was a soft invocation meant for her and her alone—a murmur carried away by the whims of the breeze, unanswered.

In the labyrinth's heart, Aurya lifted her gaze to the heavens, where the moon traced its indifferent arc. For a fleeting moment, she allowed herself the fantasy of celestial bodies locked in their dance, bound by forces greater than themselves, yet free in their orbits. And then she walked on, her footsteps a silent echo in the vastness of the garden, a testament to the complexities of an immortal love that defied both time and death.

The night wrapped its cloak around the garden, shrouding Safwan in shadows as he navigated the labyrinth of hedges. His heart was a relentless drumbeat in his chest, each thud a reminder of the urgency that propelled him forward. Moonlight fractured through the leaves, casting a silver glow on the path ahead, but Aurya's form remained elusive—a ghostly whisper just beyond reach.

"Where are you, Gem?" His voice broke the stillness, the name an old endearment that felt like a key turning in a lock long rusted. He paused, listening for the slightest rustle, the softest sigh that would signal her presence. The garden seemed to hold its breath, waiting.

Aurya's name lingered on the breeze, a siren song threading through the twisted passages. She paused, pressed against the cool embrace of an ancient yew tree. Her anger, once a blazing inferno, had cooled to smoldering embers. Safwan's voice pierced the veil of her solitude, stirring something within her that she believed to be extinguished—hope, perhaps, or the remnants of a love that refused to die.

She hesitated, the tendrils of darkness coiling around her like a lover's caress. To step out into the light was to bare her soul, to confront the myriad facets of their shared eternity—love and pain entwined so tightly that one could not exist without the other.

"Please, Aurya." The longing in Safwan's voice was raw, unguarded, a mirror to the ache that pulsed within her own breast. It was this vulnerability that drew her from the sanctuary of shadows, her figure emerging like a phantom given form.

Their eyes met across the distance—a collision of past and present, of all that was said and left unsaid. In his gaze, she read the centuries of sorrow, the weight of a crown never asked for, and the undying flame of devotion that had survived the ravages of time.

Aurya's stance was resolute, yet her dark eyes betrayed the fragility of a heart that had loved too fiercely and lost too much. They stood apart, immortal beings carved from the same stone of suffering and survival, each seeking absolution in the other's reflection.

Safwan's outstretched hand bridged the chasm of centuries, his fingers trembling as they sought the warmth of Aurya's cheek. The touch was featherlight, a whisper against her eternal pallor, laden with a remorse that eclipsed the moonlit sky. Words, once prisoners within him, cascaded forth in a torrent of yearning and regret.

"Aurya," he began, his voice a tremulous thread woven through the stillness, "my absence has carved hollows within me, shadows where your light once dwelled. For every corner of this earth that I have fled to, it was your visage that haunted me, a specter of what I had forsaken."

With each word, the garden seemed to hold its breath, the rustling leaves pausing in their nocturnal dance. The hedges stood sentinel around them, an audience to this confession that spanned lifetimes.

Aurya's gaze bore into him, two dark pools reflecting the turmoil that surged beneath her composed exterior. Her lips parted, but no sound emerged, as if the very act of speech could shatter the fragile tapestry of hope and sorrow that enveloped them.

"Every dawn that greeted me was but another reminder of the dusk I have forced upon us—a twilight of our own making. Can you forgive this wretched heart that beats solely for you?" His plea hung between them, a delicate filament shimmering with vulnerability.

She drew back slightly, the caress of his fingertips lingering like the echo of a long-forgotten melody. A solitary tear traced a glistening path down her cheek, defying the agelessness of her visage. It was a silent testament to the pain etched upon the canvas of her soul—a portrait of love immortalized by sacrifice and regret.

"Your words," she whispered, her voice threading through the space between them, "they stir something ancient within me, Safwan. A duel between the agony of remembrance and the promise of a morrow entwined with your essence."

The very air seemed saturated with the weight of their history, every whispered breeze heavy with the scent of jasmine and the salt of unshed tears. Aurya's eyes shimmered, starlight captured within their depths, as she absorbed the gravity of his confession.

"Decades have turned to dust, yet here we stand, irrevocably bound by blood and desire. Tell me, my prince, is there strength enough in your arms to rebuild what was once shattered? Do we dare dream of a future not marred by the sins of our past?"

Their immortal bond, a tapestry of intricate design, lay unraveled at their feet. In the silence that followed, the garden held its collective breath, awaiting the answer that would either weave them anew or consign their love to the annals of eternity.

The moonlight draped itself across the garden like a shroud, casting elongated shadows that danced upon the labyrinth of hedges. The whispering leaves rustled in the night's embrace, a symphony to accompany the discord of two immortal hearts. In the midst of this orchestrated stillness, Safwan reached for Aurya's hand with a deliberate gentleness that belied the turmoil raging within him.

"Look at me, Aurya," he murmured, his voice barely rising above the sighs of the sea winds that swept through the cliffsides far below. His fingers entwined with hers, the warmth of his touch a stark contrast against the coolness of her skin. "I promise you, on the remnants of our shattered trust, I will mend what has been broken. I will be the architect of our redemption if you but grant me the chance."

Aurya's gaze lingered upon their joined hands, a visual testament to years of love and torment intertwined as intricately as their fingers. The opulent ring upon her finger, a trinket from an age long past, gleamed dully under the celestial glow, its stones holding echoes of laughter and screams alike.

"Promises are but whispers against the tempest of time, my prince," she began, her voice a blend of fragility and resolve. Her eyes, pools of midnight reflecting the weight of centuries, met his as she continued, "Within this endless span, I've harbored fears deep enough to drown us both. My soul is weary, Safwan. Immortality is a crown laced with thorns, and it bleeds me dry."

Her words fell upon the night, heavy with the scent of jasmine that clung to the air like desperate spirits. Aurya's confession laid bare the chasm within her—a chasm wrought by endless days of solitude, where the specter of her own undying existence loomed large over every fleeting moment of joy.

"Each dawn I rise, and with it rises the dread of an eternity without solace," she said, her voice steady despite the storm of emotions that raged within. "You speak of rebuilding, yet the very foundations of our being are steeped in darkness. Can love truly flourish in soil sown with such despair?"

Safwan felt the weight of her words settle upon his shoulders, a burden he was determined to bear. His thumb brushed the back of her hand, a silent vow that he would weather the tempests of her soul, that together they could cultivate a garden from the wasteland of their everlasting night.

The shadows of the night seemed to recoil as Safwan stepped forward, the moon carving out his form from the darkness. His eyes, reflecting centuries of torment and tenderness, found Aurya's silhouette beside the whispering hedges. In a moment that stretched like eternity, he closed the distance between them, his movements deliberate, as if every step were an act of penance.

"Please, Aurya," he breathed, his voice no more than a murmur against the symphony of nocturnal life that thrummed around them—the distant crash of waves, the rustling leaves, the call of the nightjar—a solitary plea in the chorus of the everlasting.

His arms enfolded her with a reverence that bespoke of ancient castles and timeless vows. The contact was a spark that set their immortal essence aflame, igniting the dormant passion that had simmered beneath the ashes of their separation.

Aurya stood motionless, a marble statue come to life under Safwan's touch. Her breath hitched as she felt the familiar warmth of his embrace seep into her bones, thawing the icy solitude that had encased her heart for decades.

"Your hope..." she whispered, the vibrations of her voice barely causing a ripple in the hush of the garden. "It shines so brightly, even now, after all this time. How do you sustain it amidst such darkness?"

In their closeness, he could feel the tremors of her uncertainty mingling with the resolve that had carried her through the centuries. Safwan's chest tightened, his own fears momentarily forgotten in the wake of her quiet strength. Their bodies pressed together became a bulwark against the relentless tide of time that sought to erode their existence.

"Because I believe in us," he replied, his words imbued with a conviction that defied the very darkness they stood within. "Our love is the one thing that has endured, Aurya. It will continue to do so."

She inhaled deeply, drawing in the scent of him—sandalwood and solemnity—and with it the courage to face the labyrinthine path of their shared destiny. Aurya's arms wrapped around him, fingers tracing the contours of his back, finding solace in the solid reality of his presence.

"Then we shall endure," she proclaimed, her voice steadying as the tide inside her swelled with a hope that mirrored his. "Together, we will carve a path through this endless night. For our love is not a delicate blossom to wither in despair, but a fierce blaze that refuses to be extinguished."

In the silence that followed, their hearts spoke in silent communion, reaffirming a bond that neither time nor tragedy could sever. And there, amid the labyrinthine garden bathed in silver light, they found refuge in each other's arms, two immortal souls bound by love's undying flame.

The night unfurled its shadowy tendrils around the garden, a silent witness to the unfolding drama between two souls eternally entwined. The moon overhead bathed them in an ethereal glow, casting their elongated shadows upon the labyrinthine path that had born the weight of Aurya's solitary anguish.

Safwan, with eyes that held centuries of love and torment, gazed into Aurya's dark pools shimmering with unspoken promises. "Aurya," he began, his voice a low rumble against the quietude, "I vow to you, upon the very essence of my being, to protect you against the tempests that may come." Every syllable was a hammer striking the forge of destiny, shaping the iron-clad bonds of their immortal union. "To cherish our love" — he paused, the depth of his conviction resonating through the cool air — "as fervently as the stars cling to the obsidian sky."

She stood before him, her own eyes reflecting back the solemn oath like mirrors in the darkness. Aurya, the Gem of al-Andalus, whose beauty had once commanded empires, now found herself anchored by words that promised shelter from the relentless storm of eternity.

With the moon as their sole luminary, they stepped closer, their movements a choreography refined by time's relentless passage. It was a dance of love and redemption, every step a testament to their resilience, every turn an act of defiance against the cruel hand of fate.

Their lips met, and it was as if the heavens themselves conspired to still the earth's rotation. The kiss was not merely a union of flesh but an alchemy of souls; it was both a revelation and a homecoming. In that bittersweet communion, Aurya tasted the sorrow and the joy that had seasoned their lives, the delicate tang of immortality that cursed as much as it gifted.

Safwan's hands cradled her face, as tender as they were unwavering. Through the veil of her lashes, Aurya glimpsed the silhouette of the man who was both her downfall and her salvation. Their breath mingled, a shared zephyr in the silence of the night, while the scent of jasmine and the distant sea whispered secrets only lovers could decipher.

In this embrace, under the watchful gaze of the cosmos, they marked the beginning of a new chapter—one not confined by the pages of time, but written in the very stars that hung above. For though their flesh might never know the grace of aging, their love, boundless and profound, remained evergreen in the face of an infinite horizon.

The night air clung to them, a shroud of mist that seemed to whisper of the eons they had traversed together, each second an epoch in itself. Aurya's hand lay clasped in Safwan's, not merely as a gesture of unity but as an anchor tethering them to this moment—this decision—that felt more like destiny than choice.

Their feet tread softly upon the mossy path leading back to their grand mansion. The echo of their footfalls against the cobblestones was a rhythmic cadence, a hymn to their undying bond. Their shadows stretched long and intertwined, cast by the pallid glow of the moon hanging heavy in an obsidian sky, an eternal witness to their immortal saga.

Aurya allowed her gaze to drift over the silhouette of their home, its spires and turrets cutting into the velvet night. It was a fortress built upon the sands of time, imbued with memories of passion and strife. Her heart, a wellspring of contradictions, swelled with an emotion she dared not name—hope, perhaps, or the courage to dream of a future unmarred by the scars of their past.

Safwan's grip tightened imperceptibly, as if he sensed the tremor of her thoughts. "Together," he murmured, his voice barely rising above the whisper of the sea breeze that wove through the cliffsides. It was a vow, spoken not out of necessity but out of an understanding that spanned centuries—a shared resilience against the relentless tide of eternity.

"Always," Aurya responded, the word a solemn oath that reverberated through her being. She could feel the weight of his promise, the unwavering devotion that coursed through him, as palpable as the lifeblood they no longer needed.

They paused at the threshold of their abode, the grandeur of its façade a stark contrast to the intimacy of their exchange. The opulence that surrounded them spoke of power and prestige, yet it paled in comparison to the profundity of their connection. Here, amid the echoes of empires risen and fallen, their love remained, defiant and indomitable.

As they crossed into the embrace of their home, the door closing behind them with a sound that seemed to seal away the world, Aurya and Safwan stood united. They were two souls adrift on the endless sea of immortality, yet bound by a love as ancient as the stars. And with hands still joined, they stepped forward into the labyrinth of forever, their hearts alight with a purpose renewed by the fire of their enduring affection.

Chapter 7

غروب "Sunset"

The cobblestones whispered under their feet as Aurya and Safwan, hands clasped like woven threads of fate, drifted through the bustling market. Portugal's sun cast a golden hue upon their path, crowning the scene with an effulgent glow. Yet, even amidst the jovial clamor and vibrant tapestries of life unfurling around them, there lingered a shadow—a reminder of their eternal dance with darkness.

Aurya's gaze, dark and fathomless as the night sky from which she drew her strength, caught the glint of metal from a nearby stall. The adornments on display were not mere trinkets but relics of craftsmanship, each piece whispering tales of forgotten epochs. Among them, a silver necklace held a moon-shaped pendant that seemed to echo her own hidden luster—a beacon for her undying spirit.

"Beautiful, isn't it?" she murmured, her voice a velvet caress against the din of commerce.

Safwan, whose noble blood coursed with silent turmoil, studied the curve of Aurya's lips as they shaped her desire. Without a word, he approached the vendor, his movements deliberate and suffused with a quiet determination born of centuries of power struggles. In the exchange of coins for craftsmanship, there was a sense of loyalty—an offering to appease the restless heart of his immortal consort.

As he returned to her side, the necklace in hand, the air seemed to thrum with unspoken understanding. With each movement, the pendant caught the light, reflecting their endless journey through the ages—a testament to love's enduring flame, yet also a shackle forged by their shared torment.

"Allow me," Safwan offered, his words scarce yet laden with meaning as he fastened the necklace around Aurya's slender neck. The cool touch of silver against her skin was a sensation that defied time, a fleeting comfort against the backdrop of ceaseless wandering.

In that moment, the market around them faded into insignificance—a world apart from their own reality. They stood, two sovereigns in the realm of shadows, bound by a love that transcended mortality. And as the pendant settled against her chest, it felt like a promise, or perhaps a plea, for a peace they had yet to find.

Aurya's fingers traced the moon's crescent on her new necklace, its chill a stark contrast to the warmth radiating from Safwan's palm upon her back. She lifted her gaze, finding his eyes—a mirage of mirth and centuries-old sorrow. Gratitude shimmered within her, not just for the trinket itself, but for the constancy it represented amidst their eternal voyage through time. With a grace that belied the weight of her immortal soul, she leaned into his embrace, her lips parting in a silent whisper of thanks that was felt rather than heard.

"Every star in our night sky," Safwan murmured, the phrase as timeless as their bond. They stood, locked in an orbit of their own making, two celestial beings whose love had been both their salvation and their curse.

The market's cacophony dimmed as they wandered onwards, each step a soft echo of the lives they'd once lived. A stall draped in shadows beckoned them nearer, where ceramics painted with dreams and memories promised a glimpse of a simpler existence. The artisan's handiwork lay displayed like fragments of a world untouched by darkness—a stark reminder of their own lost humanity.

"Behold," Aurya whispered, her voice threading through the tense air as she caressed the curve of a glazed vase. Its azure hue rivaled the depth of the midday sky, while golden filigree danced across its surface like sunlight upon water.

"Such craftsmanship speaks of a life poured into art," Safwan noted, his tone laced with respect for the talent required to birth such beauty from mere clay. His gaze lingered on a platter adorned with a phoenix rising from ashes, a poignant symbol of their endless cycle of destruction and rebirth.

"Would that we could capture this moment," Aurya mused, the hint of a smile gracing her lips. "To preserve it as these artisans do with their creations."

Safwan's response came not in words but in the quiet understanding that passed between them—a silent acknowledgment of the power they wielded and the burdens it bore. As they stood amidst the pottery, surrounded by a tapestry of colors vibrant enough to rival the tapestries of old, the sense of shared history and unyielding loyalty enfolded them, as enduring as the earthenware that spanned generations yet remained ever fragile in the march of time.

Aurya leaned closer to the artisan, her dark eyes reflecting the myriad colors of his painted ceramics. "Your hands wield not merely brushes but wands," she said, her voice a soft whisper that barely rose above the murmur of the bustling market. "Each piece a testament to an unseen muse."

The artisan, a man whose age was betrayed by the wisdom in his eyes rather than the lines on his face, looked up from his work, a smile crinkling the corners of his eyes. "Ah, senhora," he began, his tone warm with the pride of a creator, "each stroke is a word in the story of my life. This," he gestured towards a bowl painted with the sea and ships, "is inspired by the tales of explorers who ventured beyond the horizon, chasing the setting sun."

Aurya and Safwan listened, enthralled as the artisan spun narratives of distant lands and ancient myths that had breathed life into his art. The man spoke of love lost at sea, of battles won and kingdoms fallen, each tale more vivid than the last. It was as though with every word, the artisan was painting invisible scenes in the air before them.

"Time may erode the mightiest empires," Aurya replied, her tone threaded with the melancholy of one who had witnessed the rise and fall of countless realms, "but your artistry captures their essence, immortalizing them forever."

"Perhaps," Safwan added softly, "it is through such creations that all of us seek to defy the relentless march of time." His words hung between them, heavy with the unspoken truth of their own ceaseless journey through the centuries.

As they turned away from the stall, Aurya's gaze caught sight of a hat woven from straw, its simplicity a stark contrast to the ornate pottery they had just admired. With a playful glint in her eye, she lifted the hat and placed it atop her flowing raven hair. She tilted her head to the side, affecting a mock pose of elegance.

"Does this suit me?" she teased, her lips curving into a mischievous smile that for a moment chased away the shadows of eternity from her features.

Safwan chuckled, the sound rich and genuine in the midst of the surrounding cacophony. "My dearest Gem," he said, his eyes dancing with amusement, "you could don a beggar's cloak and still outshine the stars themselves."

Their laughter mingled, a brief and precious melody that soared above the din of the marketplace. For an instant, the weight of their immortality seemed to lift, allowing them a fleeting semblance of humanity. It was a shared reprieve, a momentary escape from the looming specter of their endless existence, and in that instant, they were simply two souls entwined by love and laughter beneath the Iberian sun.

Emerging from the shadow of mirth, Aurya and Safwan navigated the labyrinthine market, their journey weaving through the cacophony of voices and vibrant tapestries of color that adorned the stalls. The sun, a relentless sentinel in the sky, cast its golden gaze upon the couple as they wandered. It was then that the rich, warm aroma of baking dough and sweet confections lured them towards a stall framed by an awning of crimson and gold.

"Pastéis de nata," Aurya murmured, her eyes alighting with a spark that belied the ancient soul within. Each pastry, a delicate sculpture of flaky crust and custard, seemed to whisper promises of ephemeral delight. "I must try one of each flavor," she declared, a rare playfulness touching her lips as she reached for the first of the glistening treats.

Safwan watched her, the lines of time and sorrow momentarily smoothed from his face, replaced by a tender warmth. There was something infinitely healing in witnessing Aurya's joy, a balm to the scars that marred both their hearts. As she delicately bit into a pastry, spiced cinnamon and vanilla unfurling like silken threads upon her tongue, her eyelids fluttered closed in reverence to the moment. The world around them seemed to pause, the hum of the market dimming into insignificance.

The immortal noblewoman savored the burst of flavors, each bite a symphony composed across centuries of longing for such simple pleasures. These pastries held no power, no grandeur, yet in their sweetness lay an undeniable allure—a fleeting escape from the gravity of their eternal dance with darkness.

With every morsel, Aurya allowed herself to be transported, her senses indulging in the rare gift of forgetting, if only for a heartbeat, the weight of her choices and the undying thirst that haunted her existence. She reveled in the taste of sunlight captured within the creamy texture, a testament to the mortal artisans whose hands shaped these ephemeral works of art.

"Delicious," she whispered, the word a sigh of contentment that traversed the expanse of time, echoing the countless lifetimes they had spent searching for solace in each other's arms.

Safwan remained silent, content to observe the play of emotions across Aurya's features—a portrait of complexity painted in shades of joy and wistfulness. In her pleasure, he found his own, a reflection of the love that bound them tighter than any curse ever could. Here, amidst the throngs of life that ebbed and flowed around them, they stood as timeless sentinels of an unyielding passion, their story etched into the fabric of the universe, as enduring as the stars themselves.

A haunting serenade unfurled through the market's cacophony, piercing the veil of merriment with its solitary refrain. Aurya stilled, her senses ensnared by the plaintive cry of a violin—a lament that resonated within her, as timeless as her own heartbeat. Beside her, Safwan paused, his gaze seeking the source of the melody that seemed to echo the sorrow etched upon their souls.

"Listen," Aurya murmured, her voice barely above the rustle of the crowd. "It sings of ancient grief."

Together, they moved towards the sound, drawn as moths to a mournful flame. The violinist, a mere silhouette against the stone facade, coaxed from the strings a story that spoke of love lost and the inexorable march of time. Aurya felt the melody seep into her veins, its cadence a mirror to the ebb and flow of centuries she had traversed—a requiem for all she had witnessed and wrought.

As the notes weaved their spell, Aurya reached for Safwan's hand, her touch light yet insistent. She led him into an open space amid the throng, where the cobblestones whispered secrets of bygone eras beneath their feet. With a grace born of countless nights beneath the moon's watchful eye, they began to dance, their movements a silent dialogue between eternal companions.

Around them, the world seemed to hold its breath, the bustling market hushing as onlookers gathered to witness the spectacle of two immortals locked in an ageless pas de deux. Aurya and Safwan, their bodies fluent in the language of loss and redemption, danced as though shedding the chains of their dark heritage, if only for the span of a song.

Their dance was a defiance of the cruel fate that bound them, each step a testament to their unyielding spirit. They moved with an elegance that belied the tumult raging beneath the surface—a synchronicity that spoke volumes of their shared history, of battles fought and solace found in one another's embrace.

The performance came to an end as the last note quivered in the air, relinquishing its hold on the audience. Applause erupted around them, a crescendo of appreciation for the beauty that had unfolded, but Aurya and Safwan scarcely heard it. For in that ephemeral moment, as the echoes of the violin faded into memory, they found themselves adrift on the tides of time—two souls, bound by love and tragedy, dancing to the rhythm of eternity.

Stepping away from the market's cacophony, Aurya guided Safwan into the cloistered embrace of a narrow alley, where shadows played upon the ancient stones and whispered secrets of centuries past. The hustle of the vibrant bazaar receded like the tide pulling away from the shore, leaving behind the intimate silence of two souls seeking solace in each other's arms.

Aurya turned to face Safwan, her raven hair cascading over her shoulders, a dark waterfall shimmering in the dim light that filtered through the overhead lattice. Her eyes, pools of midnight reflecting the depth of their shared eternity, locked onto his with an intensity that belied the softness of her touch as she traced the line of his jaw. His eyes, those twin beacons of sorrow and wisdom, held the spark of undying love that had endured the darkest of ages.

Here, in the seclusion of the alleyway, time seemed to bow before them, granting a reprieve from the relentless march of immortal existence. With a grace born of countless lifetimes, Safwan drew Aurya closer, his hand finding the small of her back, the other caressing her cheek, fingertips lingering on the pallor of her skin—a stark contrast to the warmth that radiated from within her.

Their lips met in a kiss that was both a whisper and a storm, a confluence of passion and tenderness that spoke volumes more than words could ever convey. It was a fierce declaration, a silent oath that bound them tighter than any spell—each kiss a rebellion against the confines of their cursed destiny.

As they parted, breaths mingling in the cool air, Aurya's smile was a sunbreak through the clouds of her usual melancholy. Safwan's gaze upon her was nothing short of adoration, a testament to the loyalty that had been forged and reforged like steel in the fires of their trials.

"Let us not forget this moment," Aurya murmured, her voice barely above a sigh, "for it is in these fleeting heartbeats that we truly live."

"Nor shall the world," Safwan replied, the barest hint of a smile playing upon his lips. "Our love is the power that defies empires, the light that outshines the stars themselves."

Hand in hand, they emerged from the alley's shadowy cocoon, stepping back into the life of the market with hearts buoyant and eyes aglow. As they walked, the clamor of commerce and the laughter of patrons became but a distant murmur. The essence of Portugal, with its golden sunlight and azure skies, enveloped them, welcoming their spirits to dance upon the breeze.

Together, Aurya and Safwan strolled, their steps unburdened, the weight of history momentarily lifted from their shoulders. The market, with all its colors and scents, faded into the tapestry of their endless journey. They moved through the streets, each step a promise, each glance a treasure, their love the compass guiding them through the labyrinth of eternity

Chapter 8

ممزق "Torn"

The echoes of their discord reverberated off the opulent walls, a symphony of torment that had become all too familiar in the grandiosity of their Calabasas mansion. Aurya's voice, a tempestuous blend of beauty and wrath, cut through the air with an edge sharp enough to draw blood. "I cannot breathe within these gilded cages any longer, Safwan! Centuries have passed, and yet here we remain, prisoners of our own making."

Safwan, whose regal bearing had weathered countless storms, stood as a bulwark against her fury. Desperation tinged his eloquent pleas like rust on ancient iron. "Aurya, my love, consider what happened in Portugal—the horror that unfolded there! We must stand together, lest we succumb to the darkness that has once again found us."

Her laughter was bitter, a lamentation for joys long since turned to ashes. "Together?" Aurya spat the word as though it were poison. "We are but phantoms haunting each other's eternity, bound by chains forged from misbegotten deeds."

In the privacy of the chamber that had witnessed moments both tender and tumultuous, Aurya's trembling hands betrayed the turmoil raging within her immortal soul. Garments—silk and satin whispers of lives lived in epochs now relegated to history—were folded with meticulous care, an act of defiance as much as necessity. The room seemed to contract around her, every sumptuous detail a reminder of the opulence that suffocated rather than soothed.

Her chest heaved with shallow breaths, a marionette's mimicry of life, as she placed each relic of her existence into the suitcase—a modern-day sarcophagus for memories she wished to inter. The clasp clicked shut with a finality that resonated deep in her bones, a grim echo of the tomb entrances she'd passed in lifetimes past.

"Is this the freedom you seek, Gem?" Safwan's voice broke the near-silence, fraying at the edges with anguish. "To flee from our shared fate?"

"Freedom," she whispered, the word a ghost on her lips. Her gaze lingered on him, the prince who had become both her sanctuary and her prison. "Yes, freedom from this endless night. Even shadows yearn for the dawn, Safwan."

With each article secured, Aurya felt the weight of centuries begin to lift, an ephemeral promise of release from the undying vigil they kept. The tension in the room stretched taut, a bowstring moments from snapping, threatening to unleash the arrows of their discontent upon the world once more.

Aurya stood before Safwan, her silhouette framed by the grandeur of their opulent Calabasas estate. Her eyes, once the bastion of warmth and allure, now bore the weight of an eternity's sorrow. She regarded him with a gaze that was resolute, the decision etched in the depths of her soul.

"Safwan," she said, her voice low and steady, "I cannot stay. This existence... it is a gilded cage."

"Please, Aurya." Safwan's plea was laced with desperation. He reached out to her, his hand hovering just shy of her arm as though afraid to shatter an illusion. "We have overcome much.

Think of what we endured after Portugal, the horror we left behind—"

"Which only proves my point," she interrupted, stepping back from his touch. "We are bound to repeat our tragedies, endlessly."

"Aurya, we are power and eternity entwined. What more could you want?" His words hung between them, each syllable a testament to his own imprisonment in hope.

"More?" Her laugh was hollow, a melody void of joy. "I want less, Safwan. Less of this everlasting night. I crave the dawn, even if it is one I shall never witness."

"Then let me be your sunrise," he implored, his noble visage etched with pain.

"Even the sun must set," Aurya whispered, turning away from him, her heart heavy with the price of her freedom.

With each step she took toward the exit, the shadows cast by the California sun grew longer, stretching out like fingers trying to pull her back into the darkness. Her stride was unwavering, a silent testament to the centuries of resolve hardened within her.

The mansion's doors opened to an expanse of sky, a canvas painted with the promise of infinity. Yet, today it felt different to Aurya—today, it was an escape. The light enveloped her, its radiance a stark contrast to the cool refuge she had known for so long. She paused on the threshold, allowing herself a single moment to drink in the sweet, opulent air that tasted faintly of jasmine and regret.

Safwan's figure loomed in the doorway, a sentinel against the backdrop of finery they had built together. His eyes followed her every movement, silently begging for a change of heart that would not come. But Aurya's steps did not falter; she walked forward, the sun's embrace sealing her departure, casting a coronet of light upon her raven hair.

She did not look back as she descended the steps, leaving Safwan to grapple with the echoes of their immortality in the silence of their once shared sanctuary. The door closed with a soft click, a subtle yet poignant end to an ageless chapter.

The world outside beckoned, and Aurya, the eternal Gem of al-Andalus, stepped into the unfamiliar brightness of a day without end, her future unwritten and vast before her.

Aurya's silhouette cut a sharp contrast against the golden hue of the descending sun as she navigated the rugged terrain leading to the cliffs. The untamed beauty of the California coastline unfolded before her, an expanse of raw power that mirrored the tumult within her immortal soul. Her stride was purposeful, yet each step towards the precipice was a dance with uncertainty.

The ocean below roared its timeless anthem, waves crashing against the rocks in a cacophony of natural fury. Aurya stood at the edge, where earth yielded to abyss, and gazed out over the vastness of the Pacific. The wind, wild and unyielding, whipped through her raven-black hair, tugging at her clothes like the fingers of fate beckoning her onwards.

She could feel the pulse of the world, the heartbeat of eternity in the spray of saltwater that kissed her face. The horizon blurred into the sky, a line once clear now smudged by the tears of gods or perhaps the sorrow of a woman who had seen empires rise and fall.

Drawing a deep breath that filled her lungs with the briny scent of freedom, Aurya reached into the folds of her coat, her fingers wrapping around the familiar shape of a pen. With it came a small piece of paper, creased from being folded and unfolded countless times as if the act could somehow delay the inevitable.

Her hand trembled not from the chill of the wind but from the gravity of what she was about to do. She placed the paper against the rough bark of a lone cypress tree that clung to the cliffside as tenaciously as she clung to her decision.

"Fly," she wrote, the ink stark against the parchment, a singular word heavy with the weight of centuries and the lightness of possibility. The cryptic message held a universe of meaning, a command, a plea, a release—all entwined like the roots of the tree against which she leaned.

The note fluttered slightly in the breeze as she tucked it beneath a small stone, a silent testament to the resolve in her heart. In that moment, Aurya Alcazar was both a force to be reckoned with and a specter of vulnerability—a paradox wrapped in the enigma of her own being.

She took one last look at the note, her dark eyes reflecting the dying light, and turned away from the cliff, the very edge of her old life. There was no fanfare, no flourish—only the sound of the waves, indifferent to her plight, and the quiet rustle of leaves that whispered tales of immortality to a world that never truly understood their burden.

As Aurya vanished into the burgeoning twilight, the cliff stood sentinel to the choice made, a witness to the birth of a journey that had no map, for it was charted in the constellations of her soul.

The house was still, a mausoleum to their love. Safwan stood alone in the center of the grand foyer, his gaze locked onto the small stone on the marble table that wasn't meant to be there. The note beneath it lay unfolded, a single word etched upon it that seemed to pulse with life: "Fly." His hands trembled as they reached out, the parchment feeling like both a verdict and a riddle. This one word, from her hand, clawed at the edges of his understanding, leaving him adrift in a sea of questions.

"Fly?" he murmured to the shadows, his voice barely above a whisper. The opulence of their Calabasas home mocked him now, its splendor hollow without Aurya's presence. The cryptic message was a siren's song, luring him into the depths of confusion and fear. He turned it over in his mind, searching for meaning in its simplicity. Was it a command? A plea? Or perhaps an omen of things to come?

Safwan moved through the echoing halls, each step amplifying the silence around him. The lush tapestries on the walls seemed to absorb his desperation, their threads woven with the same darkness that now threatened to consume him. The air was thick with the scent of jasmine, a fragrance that once signified home but now served as a reminder of what he feared to lose.

"Where are you, Gem?" he called out, though he knew there would be no answer. His voice, usually so sure, cracked under the weight of sudden solitude. The echoes returned to him empty-handed, carrying only the ghost of his own voice. The emptiness of the rooms loomed large, a vastness that mirrored the void within him.

He roamed each chamber, memories bleeding into the present. Here, a grand piano untouched since their last duet; there, a painting of a sunset much like the one they'd witnessed in al-Andalus centuries ago. It all felt like an elaborate stage set, props in a play where the lead actress had taken her final bow, leaving the stage bare.

In the study, books lay open, their pages whispering tales of immortality and power struggles that now felt too close to home. Safwan ran his fingers over the spines, tracing the titles that spoke of loyalty and betrayal, love and loss—fables reflecting their reality. He could almost hear Aurya's voice, reading aloud passages that resonated with their eternal struggle.

"Immortality," he scoffed, the irony not lost upon him. To live forever yet feel the sting of such profound emptiness. What good was eternity if it meant facing it alone?

He paused at the threshold of their bedroom, heart pounding against the cage of his ribs. The bed, unmade, bore the indent of her form—a haunting imprint. Safwan's breath hitched as he approached, half-expecting her to reappear, an apparition born from his deepest yearnings.

"Please," he whispered to the lingering traces of her perfume, a blend of mystery and allure that was undeniably Aurya. But only silence greeted him, a silence punctuated by the distant crash of waves against the cliffside, indifferent to his plight.

Realization settled upon him like a shroud. She was gone. The truth of it sliced through the veneer of hope he had clung to. His immortal heart, which had survived battles and betrayals, now faced a new adversary—the specter of life without her.

"Fly," she had written. And so, he must. But to where? How does one chase the wind, capture the essence of a spirit as wild and untamed as Aurya Alcazar?

Safwan stepped back into the foyer, the note still clutched in his hand. The cold light of dawn began to seep through the windows, casting long shadows across the floor. In the cruel clarity of morning, he understood that this was not an end but the beginning of a search that might span lifetimes.

"Fly," he repeated, resolve hardening within him. If she sought freedom, then he would seek her. For in the pursuit of her soul across time and space, perhaps he would find his own liberation—or at least the promise of their entwined destinies unfolding anew.

Safwan stood motionless, the abandoned halls of their California home echoing with the ghost of Aurya's departure. The grandeur of the opulent surroundings felt like a mausoleum now, hollow and cold, the air thick with the scent of loss. He let the note slip from his fingers, watching it drift to the marble floor, where it lay like a fallen leaf.

The silence was oppressive, a suffocating blanket that seemed to absorb the very essence of his being. Safwan closed his eyes, a single tear tracking down his cheek. Centuries of existence, of dominance and survival, had not prepared him for this solitary abyss. The iron in his soul bent beneath the weight of her absence; acceptance was a bitter draught to swallow.

"Fly," she had written. And fly he must, but not in pursuit. He had anchored her for too long, tethered her spirit to an earth that no longer welcomed their kind. With a weary sigh, he turned away from the life they had shared, from the memories etched into every corner of this empty palace.

As the sun cast its first golden rays over the cliffs, a figure stood alone, poised at the edge of eternity. Aurya's dark hair billowed around her like a raven's wings unfurled, her pale skin almost luminescent against the backdrop of the dawn sky. She spread her arms wide, embracing the expanse of the ocean before her, its vastness mirroring the freedom that beckoned.

The wind caressed her face, salty and invigorating, whispering the secrets of the world below. She inhaled deeply, savoring the taste of liberation on her tongue. In this moment, perched between the land and the endless blue, Aurya felt the chains of immortality begin to dissolve.

She leaned forward, her heart pounding with a fervor she hadn't known since her mortal days. The waves roared their approval as she surrendered to their call. Gravity claimed her, and she fell with grace, a meteor streaking through the morning light. The cold embrace of the waters below was a shock, a vivid reminder of life's fleeting nature.

Aurya emerged, gasping, her senses alive with the thrill of rebirth. As the currents swirled around her, carrying her towards an uncertain future, she realized that the leap was but the first step of a journey unbound by time or fate. With each stroke, she moved further from the world she knew, driven by an insatiable desire to rediscover herself beyond the confines of eternity.

Aurya staggered ashore, each step a laborious conquest against the tug of the sea. Her exquisite gown clung to her like a second skin, heavy with the ocean's grasp. Sand granules scraped at her feet as she trudged forward, the hem of her once-elegant attire tracing erratic patterns in her wake. The California coast sprawled before her, its familiar contours unchanged despite the passage of time—a cruel reminder of her perpetual existence.

The relentless sun bore down upon her pallid skin, its rays impotent against her immortal flesh yet mocking her with the illusion of warmth. Aurya's dark eyes swept over the landscape, the towering cliffs a silent sentinel to her centuries of solitude. Here, the opulence of Calabasas was a distant memory, replaced by the stark reality of nature's indifference. The gulls cried above, indifferent to her plight, their shrill voices slicing through the hush of the waves.

With every labored stride, Aurya felt the weight of countless dawns and dusks that had come before, an endless cycle from which she yearned to break free. Angst coiled within her, a serpent gnawing at the edges of resolve. The taste of salt lingered on her lips, not from the ocean's spray but from the tears she could no longer shed.

Turning her back to the sea, she set her jaw against the grief that clawed at her insides. The wind whipped her raven hair into wild tendrils, obscuring her vision as if urging her to forget the path behind. Yet, even as she moved away from the water's edge, the ghostly echoes of Safwan's pleas haunted her steps, a litany of love and desperation woven into the very air.

Ahead lay the vast expanse of the beach, its golden sands untouched by the turmoil in her heart. Aurya's form diminished with each step, the enormity of the world swallowing her whole. The horizon called to her with its siren song of obscurity, promising solace in anonymity.

Gradually, her silhouette blurred, merging with the mirage where sky kissed earth. Smaller and smaller she became, until she was nothing more than a speck on the canvas of eternity. The chapter closed with the whisper of her name carried away by the breeze, leaving behind the question of her fate hanging in the atmosphere, a lingering note of uncertainty and anticipation for what lay beyond the horizon for both Aurya and Safwan.

Chapter 9

الناسك "The Hermit"

Safwan's silhouette merged with the shadows as he traversed the labyrinthine corridors of an ancient library in al-Andalus. The weight of centuries lay heavy on his shoulders, a constant reminder of the curse that was both his power and his prison. With each step, the soft echo of his footsteps reverberated against stone walls, mingling with the distant hush of sea waves crashing against the rugged cliffs outside.

The moon, a pale specter in the sky, filtered through stained glass, casting a kaleidoscope of colors upon the dusty tomes that lined the towering shelves. Safwan's piercing eyes, reflecting centuries of wisdom and sorrow, scanned the spines of ancient texts, searching for a whisper of mortality in their silent company. His fingers, long and dexterous despite his ageless state, traced the leather bindings with a reverence reserved for sacred relics.

He selected a volume bound in faded velvet, its pages yellowed with the passage of time. The air was thick with the musk of aging paper and ink, a scent that stirred memories of a life once lived under the sun's warm embrace. Safwan settled into the solitude of a shadowed alcove, the only sound the rhythmic turning of pages as he delved into the lore of his own kind.

The library, a vault of forgotten knowledge, spoke to him in hushed tones. Here, in the heart of al-Andalus, where the sea's eternal lament whispered secrets to those patient enough to listen, Safwan sought the answers that eluded him through the ages. He pored over accounts of vampires, of immortality's cruel jest, each legend a piece of the puzzle he desperately needed to solve.

In the margins of a tattered scroll, a tale unfolded of a vampire who had challenged the gods, seeking to reclaim his mortality. Safwan's hand trembled as he scribbled notes, the connection between this myth and his plight igniting a spark of hope within his weary soul. It was a dangerous spark, one that could easily be snuffed out by the winds of despair, but it was all he had left to cling to.

As dawn threatened to breach the horizon, Safwan remained ensconced in the library's embrace, surrounded by whispers of immortality. With each account he studied, each legend he dissected, the path before him grew more treacherous, yet he pressed on, driven by an unyielding desire to be free from the endless night that was his existence.

The library's ancient stones seemed to lean in closer, as if eager to witness the outcome of Safwan's quest—a prince of darkness seeking the light of mortality, a paradox wrapped in the enigma of time. And as the first rays of dawn stretched across the land, painting the sky with hues of hope and renewal, Safwan closed the final tome with a soft thud, his resolve hardened.

His journey had only just begun.

Safwan's fingers traced the brittle edges of a parchment, his heart racing as the fragmented symbols whispered promises from the shadowed past. The scent of ancient leather and musty paper hung heavy in the air, mingling with the brine of the distant sea that clawed at the shores of al-Andalus. He leaned closer, the candlelight casting an eerie dance upon the words that held the key to his salvation—or his ultimate demise.

"An incantation," he murmured to himself, each syllable a fragile hope. The text spoke of a ritual, forbidden and fraught with peril, capable of severing the chains of immortality that had bound him for centuries. But the cost was veiled in ambiguity, a terrible price that lurked behind veils of allegory, daring him to unveil its truth.

Determined, Safwan closed the tome with a thud that echoed through the silence of the library. He rose, his athletic frame moving with an unnerving grace, a specter amongst the shelves. His resolve was unshakable; he would unearth this secret, no matter the sacrifice required.

The sun dipped below the horizon as Safwan ventured forth, seeking the guidance of one versed in ancient lore. The name whispered on the lips of erudite circles was Professor Hiroshi Tanaka, a scholar whose life's work was dedicated to unraveling the threads of myth and superstition that wove through history's tapestry.

Safwan traversed the mountains of 1920s Japan, where the old home of the professor loomed, shrouded in mist and the relentless patter of seasonal rains. The rhythmic beat of the downpour pulsed like a heartbeat through the night, as if nature itself anticipated the gravity of the meeting that was to unfold.

Within the dimly lit study, walls lined with books that bore the weight of forgotten knowledge, Safwan stood before the professor. The air was thick with the scent of ink and wet earth, a stark contrast to the dry, familiar halls he had left behind.

"Professor Tanaka," Safwan began, his voice betraying none of the turmoil that churned within him. "I have come to seek your expertise on a matter most... unusual."

The professor peered at him, eyes sharp and discerning, then gestured to a seat across from his cluttered desk. "Speak, Prince

Safwan. For I know who—and what—you are. Your reputation precedes you, even here."

A chill ran down Safwan's spine at the acknowledgment of his true nature. It was a risk to reveal himself so, but desperation drove him beyond caution. With measured breaths, he recounted his findings, watching the scholar's face for signs of recognition or fear.

"An incantation exists," Safwan confessed, the weight of his confession hanging between them. "One potent enough to strip an immortal of their curse. You are my last hope to find it and wield its power."

Professor Tanaka leaned back, the lines of his face etched with contemplation. "Such knowledge is not sought without consequence, Prince. To meddle with forces beyond mortal ken is to invite calamity."

"Calamity already shadows my every step," Safwan replied, a hint of bitterness creeping into his tone. "What more have I to lose?"

Their gazes locked, a silent battle of wills unfolding in the space of heartbeats. Finally, the professor nodded, his decision made beneath the storm's watchful eye.

"Very well. If such an incantation exists, we shall endeavor to uncover it together. Prepare yourself, Prince Safwan, for the path you choose is fraught with darkness more profound than the eternal night you wish to escape."

The promise of dawn seemed a world away as Safwan nodded, accepting the scholar's terms. Together, they would delve into the abyss of ancient secrets, where the flickering light of hope struggled against the encroaching tides of despair. And in the heart of the tempest, Safwan's quest for mortality would either be fulfilled or forever dashed upon the cliffs of futility.

The heavy scent of ancient parchment and burning incense filled the air, mingling with the tension that hung thick between Safwan and the scholar. Professor Tanaka's eyes, wide with equal parts trepidation and exhilaration, flickered over the vampire prince's solemn visage.

"An incantation of such magnitude," the professor murmured, his voice barely rising above the crackling hearth, "to undo what has been etched into the very essence of your being... It is a discovery that defies centuries of belief."

Safwan's chest tightened, a mixture of fear and desperate hope constricting around his heart like a vice. "A discovery that I am willing to pursue to its end," he affirmed, his words a silent vow.

With a slow nod, Professor Tanaka conceded, "I will aid you in this endeavor, Prince Safwan. The annals of history may yet be rewritten by our hands."

Their pact sealed with a sense of foreboding gravity, they set forth to gather the arcane components required for the ritual. The list was as peculiar as it was precise: a vial of blood from a creature untouched by moonlight, petals from a flower that bloomed only under the eclipse, and the ash of a tree struck by lightning.

Under the veiled secrecy of twilight, Safwan and the professor ventured to a secluded location known only to those who dared to whisper of its existence—a clearing ensconced within the mountains of Japan, where the cacophony of the city was but a distant memory. Here, enveloped by the whispers of the forest and shielded from prying eyes, they would invoke the incantation.

The clouds overhead brooded with an impending storm, their dark forms a testament to the unnatural forces they were about to beckon. With each step upon the damp earth, Safwan felt the weight of centuries upon his shoulders, the yearning for mortality growing more fervent within his undead heart.

"Are we not tempting fate?" Professor Tanaka asked, his voice betraying the first signs of doubt as they arranged the materials upon an ancient stone altar.

"Fate," Safwan replied, his gaze fixed upon the horizon where the last remnants of daylight fought against the encroaching darkness, "has long been a cruel mistress to me. What is there left for her to take?"

As the final preparations were made, the world seemed to hold its breath, the wind ceasing its mournful howl through the trees. In the stillness, Safwan's thoughts turned to Aurya, her image a beacon of light in the oppressive gloom that threatened to suffocate him. For her, for a chance at redemption, he would face whatever horrors lay ahead.

"Let us begin," Professor Tanaka declared, and with a somber determination, they stepped into the circle of power they had wrought, ready to challenge the immutable laws of nature in pursuit of an elusive dream: to live, to die, to be, at last, free.

The shadows lengthened around Safwan and Professor Tanaka, creeping closer as if drawn by the gravity of their endeavor. Above them, the canopy of ancient trees swayed gently, whispering secrets to the stars that had begun to emerge in the twilight sky. The world around them was a tapestry woven with the threads of pending darkness and fading light, and within it, they stood at the precipice of the unknown.

Professor Tanaka's voice rose, a sonorous incantation that seemed to resonate with the very air itself. His hands moved with precision, tracing esoteric symbols that hung momentarily in the charged atmosphere before dissipating like smoke. Each uttered syllable was a key, each gesture a turn of the lock in the vault of eternity.

Safwan's pulse thrummed in his ears, a rhythmical counterpoint to the scholar's chant. His breath came in shallow drafts, anticipation tightening his chest until he felt he could draw no more air. It was here, this moment, that held the fragile promise of an end—a terminus to the ceaseless march of his immortal days.

The air grew thick, heavy with power that crackled and arced between the stones of the altar. Time seemed to bend, to fold upon itself under the weight of ancient magic now awakened. Safwan's eyes, once accustomed to piercing through the darkest nights, now watched the scene through a haze of otherworldly energies that swirled and converged upon him.

"Let it be done," Professor Tanaka intoned, his voice reaching a crescendo that shook the leaves from their branches and sent a shiver through the earth beneath them.

Safwan braced for the impact, for the shattering transformation that would strip away the curse of centuries. He envisioned the sun warming his skin without the threat of destruction, the sweet release of a final rest that had eluded him for so long.

But there was no shattering, no seismic shift in the fabric of his being. Instead, a hollow quiet descended, a silence so profound that it seemed as though the world had withdrawn its breath. The energy dissipated, leaving behind only the scent of ozone and a chilling absence.

He opened his eyes, the eternal sharpness of his gaze now clouded by disbelief. Before him, the ritual site lay undisturbed, the scholar's hands still poised in the last motion of the spell. Around them, the night resumed its natural chorus, oblivious to the failed alchemy that had sought to defy its immutable laws.

"Impossible," Safwan whispered, the word tasting of ash on his tongue. The hope that had kindled within him, bright and beckoning, was extinguished, snuffed out by the cruel hand of failure. Desolation settled over him, a mantle heavier than any regal cloak he had ever borne.

The scholar, his face etched with confusion and regret, met Safwan's gaze. "I... I don't understand," he stammered, the confidence of his scholarly authority reduced to the tremulous uncertainty of a frightened child.

"Nor do I," Safwan replied, his eloquence abandoned in the face of crushing disappointment. The allure of mortality, once so tantalizingly close, now retreated into the realm of fantasy, leaving him to grapple with the reality of his endless existence.

In the wake of the broken incantation, Safwan stood amidst the ruins of his dreams, a prince of darkness bound to the night, his quest for salvation lying in tatters at his feet.

Darkness clung to the room, a silent witness to Safwan's fury. His hands clenched into fists at his sides, the knuckles white as the moon that shone with impotent serenity outside the old home nestled in the mountains of 1920s Japan. The scholar recoiled, his back pressing against the cold wall, the scrolls and texts that had promised so much lay scattered and trampled beneath Safwan's feet.

"Speak!" Safwan commanded, his voice a low growl that resonated with suppressed wrath. "Why did your incantations fail? What truth have you concealed from me?"

The scholar, his eyes wide with terror, struggled to find his voice. He had never seen such an embodiment of menace, not even in the darkest of folklore he'd studied. "There... there might be conditions... factors unaccounted for..." he stuttered, his words stumbling over each other in their haste to escape.

"Conditions?" Safwan echoed, the word slicing through the thick air like a blade. His heart was a drumbeat of desperation, driving him to the brink of madness. "What conditions? You assured me of your knowledge!"

"Legends... they are not always complete," the scholar whispered, shrinking before the towering figure of the immortal prince. "There could be elements lost to time, keys to the spell that we... that I do not know."

Safwan's breath came in shallow gasps as his anger swelled, consuming the last vestiges of his control. In his mind's eye, centuries of night stretched out before him, each one a mocking echo of the life he yearned to live—to age, to perish, to rest. But it was all slipping away, unraveling like the threads of the very scrolls that promised him freedom.

"Useless," he spat out, the word laced with venom. And then, without a thought, without a plan, his hand shot out, propelled by the force of his rage. It found the scholar's throat, gripping it with a strength that knew no bounds, no mortality.

"Please..." the scholar choked out, his hands clawing at Safwan's iron grasp, his eyes pleading for mercy that would not—could not—come.

But it was too late. The realization crashed into Safwan like a wave against the cliffs of al-Andalus, cold and relentless. The scholar's body went limp, a ragdoll in the arms of the monster Safwan had become.

"No," Safwan breathed, releasing his hold as if burned. The scholar crumpled to the floor, a heap of wasted potential and lost knowledge. The silence that followed was deafening, broken only by the distant wail of the typhoon winds that mourned outside.

Safwan stood alone, the weight of eternity bearing down upon him once again. The scholar's unseeing eyes gazed up at him, a mirror reflecting the horror of what he had done—the irreversible act of a being caught between power and fragility, loyalty and betrayal, life and the endless void of immortality.

His hands trembled as he looked upon the destruction wrought by his own hands, the scholar's final breath lingering in the air, a testament to the futility of their struggle against fate. In that moment, the prince of darkness realized that his search for salvation was nothing more than a chase after shadows, a battle against an enemy that could never be vanquished.

The storm outside wailed a dirge for the dead, its lamentations weaving through the cracks of the old mountain home. Inside, Prince Safwan stood motionless, the echo of his wrath still ringing in the hollow chamber of his heart. The scholar's blood was a stark contrast against the weathered floorboards, a crimson stain spreading like the dawn of a day that would never come for him.

Safwan's breaths came in shallow gasps, each one a shudder that wracked his immortal frame. Guilt clawed at his insides, sharper than any blade forged by human hands. He had sought to unshackle himself from the chains of eternity, but now he was fettered by remorse, his hands forever stained by the life he had snuffed out so thoughtlessly.

In the eerie silence that followed the tempest of his rage, Safwan's mind spun with phantoms of the past. He saw the faces of those whose lives he had taken, heard the whispers of their unfulfilled destinies. The scholar had been a beacon of hope, and now he lay extinguished, another victim in Safwan's cursed existence.

The weight of centuries pressed upon Safwan's shoulders as he turned away from the body, his gaze lost to the shadows that clung to the corners of the room. With faltering steps, he retreated, the once proud prince reduced to a specter fleeing the scene of his own crime.

He wandered into solitude, the oppressive darkness of the night matching the void expanding within him. The sweet scent of jasmine from far-off lands mingled with the damp earthiness of his surroundings, a cruel reminder of the world's beauty that he could no longer appreciate without the bitter tinge of his endless sorrow.

Safwan found refuge in an alcove shielded from the relentless downpour, the cold stone a fitting throne for a king of desolation. There, amidst the relentless fury of the typhoon, he contemplated the ironies of his existence—endowed with the power to defy death, yet powerless to reclaim his humanity.

"Is there no respite?" he murmured to the uncaring wind, his voice barely rising above a whisper. "No end to this accursed immortality?"

But the storm offered no answers, only the incessant drumming of rain against the earth, a rhythm as eternal as Safwan's own heartbeat.

There, in the heart of the tempest, Safwan surrendered to the realization that his quest might be as boundless as the sea that raged below the cliffs of al-Andalus. Perhaps his fate was to chase the horizon forever, always seeking, never finding the solace of mortality.

He closed his eyes, listening to the symphony of nature's indifference—the ultimate requiem for a prince who had become a prisoner of time.

Safwan's fingertips grazed the ancient amulet hanging from his neck, its surface as cold as the unyielding march of time. He paced within the narrow confines of the alcove, each step an echo of his inner turmoil. The relentless rain outside was a cacophony that tried to drown out his thoughts, but it only sharpened the edge of his contemplation.

The heavy air clung to him like a shroud, and he felt the weight of centuries pressing against his chest. He had lived through epochs, witnessed empires rise and crumble into dust, yet the answer to his curse eluded him still. Safwan's existence, once adorned with the splendor of royal courts, now mirrored the stark, barren landscape that stretched beyond his shelter.

In the tempest's deafening howl, he heard the whispers of history, taunting him with the promise of death—a promise that was never meant for him. The irony of his plight wrapped around his heart, squeezing tighter than the coils of a serpent. He had longed for release, sought it in forbidden texts and dark incantations, only to find himself further ensnared in the web of immortality.

"Is this my penance?" he questioned the shadows that danced upon the walls, their forms distorted and fleeting. "To be forever caught between dusk and dawn, never to greet the final sunset?"

A flash of lightning illuminated the rugged terrain outside, casting jagged silhouettes that seemed to mock his predicament. Each bolt was a testament to nature's indifferent might, and Safwan knew well the futility of battling forces greater than oneself.

Yet, surrender did not come easily to a prince who had once commanded armies. The same blood that had spurred him to greatness now coursed with a stubborn resolve. Safwan's mind reeled with the memories of Aurya—her laughter, her touch, the way she made him feel alive even as they both existed beyond life's natural reach.

"Must I abandon hope?" he whispered into the void, the question a fragile thing, frail against the onslaught of eternity.

He thought of the scholar, a life extinguished by his own hand, a casualty in a war against an unyielding adversary. Guilt gnawed at his soul, a reminder that his quest came at a cost far too dear. Could he justify further sacrifice in pursuit of an end that might never come?

With a weary sigh, Safwan pressed his palm against the rough stone wall, feeling its ancient strength. It stood resolute, a silent sentinel bearing witness to the passage of ages. In that moment, he envied the simplicity of rock and rain—they did not yearn; they simply were.

"Perhaps there is no deliverance," he conceded, the words tasting of defeat. "Maybe some fates are written in stone, unchangeable as the course of the stars."

But as the storm raged on, Safwan's heart rebelled against acceptance. He could no more deny the pull of his desire for an end than he could stop the earth from turning. And so, he remained caught in the throes of indecision, a man torn between the relentless tide of his longing and the stark cliffs of reality.

The chapter closed with Safwan standing solitary amidst the fury of nature, his gaze fixed on the horizon that hid the secrets of life and death. His internal conflict raged as fiercely as the typhoon outside, an immortal enigma wrestling with the specter of an eternal tomorrow.

Chapter 10

‏الإصدار الحلو‏ ‏ا‏ "Sweet Release"

The moon shone brightly over London, casting its silver light on the cobblestone streets. From a phone booth tucked away in an alley, Safwan nervously clutched the handset, his long fingers tapping an erratic rhythm against the plastic as he waited for the scholar to pick up. He had spent decades searching for someone who might hold the key to breaking the curse that tethered him and Aurya to immortality.

"Hello?" The voice on the other end was cautious but curious, and Safwan felt his cold heart quicken with hope.

"Dr. Wren? My name is Safwan, and I have been researching the folklore surrounding the curse of eternal life," he began, his voice low and steady. "I believe I have found something that could help break it—an incantation—but I need your expertise."

"Interesting," Dr. Wren said, her tone betraying her fascination. "I'm quite familiar with the legends, but I must admit this is the first time anyone has contacted me about them. What makes you think this incantation will work?"

"Because," Safwan paused, gathering his courage, "I am cursed myself. I am a vampire." There was silence on the line, and for a moment, he feared he'd gone too far. But then the scholar spoke again, her voice tinged with a thrill that mirrored his own desperation.

"Remarkable. And you truly believe this incantation can save you?" she asked, her skepticism giving way to intrigue.

"More than anything, Dr. Wren," Safwan replied earnestly. "But I cannot do it alone. Will you help me?"

"Alright," she agreed after a moment's thought. "We should meet to discuss this further. Somewhere private."

"An abandoned church near St. James's Park," Safwan suggested, knowing the place well from countless nights spent in quiet contemplation. "It's secluded, and no one ever goes there."

"Very well," Dr. Wren said, her voice filled with determination. "Tomorrow night at midnight. I'll be there."

"Thank you," Safwan whispered, his undead heart swelling with a strange mixture of hope and dread. As he hung up the phone, he couldn't help but wonder what price he would have to pay for this chance at redemption.

The moon hung low in the sky, casting an eerie silver glow over the abandoned church as Safwan approached. The sharp steeple pierced the night like a dagger, and he couldn't help but feel as if it were a symbol of his own tormented soul. As he pushed open the heavy wooden doors, the smell of damp stone and decay enveloped him, a testament to the passage of time that had all but forgotten this place.

"Dr. Wren?" he called into the darkness, his voice echoing through the empty pews. He was greeted by the soft rustle of footsteps, and then she stepped into the circle of moonlight, her eyes alight with curiosity.

"Mr. Safwan," she said, extending her hand for a brief handshake. "It's a pleasure to finally meet you."

"Likewise," Safwan replied, his mind racing with the knowledge that his fate might rest in this woman's hands. "Thank you for coming."

"Of course," she said, her gaze sweeping the crumbling walls. "It's not every day one meets a vampire seeking redemption."

"Then let's not waste any more time," Safwan urged, feeling the burning weight of his immortality bearing down on him. "Tell me what you know about the curse."

"Very well," Dr. Wren agreed, her scholarly demeanor taking over. She pulled out a tattered notebook from her satchel, her fingers brushing over the worn pages with reverence. "As I'm sure you're aware, the curse of vampirism has been chronicled in various forms throughout history. Often, these stories are dismissed as mere superstitions, but there is a common thread: the belief that those cursed can regain their humanity through an ancient incantation."

Safwan listened intently, his heart pounding in his chest despite the stillness of his undead body. "What do the legends say about the consequences of breaking the curse?"

"Ah, that's where things become more...troubling," Dr. Wren replied, her brow furrowing as she flipped through her notes. "Many accounts suggest that there is a terrible price to be paid for undoing the curse. Some speak of unimaginable pain, while others recount tales of a life for a life – someone close to the cursed individual must die in order for them to regain their humanity."

Safwan's breath caught in his throat at the mention of Aurya, and he could feel the cold tendrils of fear wrapping around his heart. But as he looked into Dr. Wren's eyes, filled with determination and knowledge, he knew he had no choice but to press on. For both their sakes, he had to try.

A single candle flickered, casting dancing shadows upon the walls of the dimly lit room. The scent of old parchment filled the air as Safwan leaned forward, his gaze locked on Dr. Wren's steady hands as she leafed through her notes.

"Tell me more about this incantation," Safwan implored, his voice barely above a whisper. His eyes betrayed the desperation he tried to keep hidden. "What must I do to perform it?"

Dr. Wren hesitated, her fingers pausing mid-turn. She looked up from her research, concern weighing heavy in her eyes. "Safwan, I must warn you – the dangers of meddling with ancient magic cannot be overstated. There are few who have attempted such spells and come away unscathed."

"Yet, here I am," Safwan replied, his jaw set with determination. "Centuries spent searching for answers, hoping against hope that there might be a way to break free from this curse."

The scholar studied Safwan's face, taking in the lines carved by centuries of torment, the desperate glint in his once-vibrant eyes. She sighed, relenting. "I understand your desperation, Safwan. And I will help you. But you must promise me that you are prepared for the potential consequences, whatever they may be."

Safwan nodded, clenching his fists in silent resolve. He already knew the price might be steep, but the prospect of reclaiming his humanity and freeing Aurya was worth any cost. "I'm ready," he whispered.

"Very well." Dr. Wren turned her attention back to her notes, her voice low and measured as she began to explain the intricacies of the ritual. "The incantation requires a series of specific components – elements that represent both life and death, as well as the essence of the vampire curse itself."

"Such as?" Safwan asked, committing each word to memory.

"Blood of the cursed, for one," she replied. "The earth from a grave of one who fell victim to the curse, and a sprig of hawthorn – a symbol of protection against evil spirits."

Safwan listened, his heart pounding with a mixture of fear and determination. He knew that the path he was about to embark on could lead to salvation or utter destruction, but there was no turning back now.

The moon hung low in the sky, casting an eerie glow over the abandoned churchyard. The wind whispered through the branches of the ancient trees, as though the spirits of the past were murmuring their secrets. Safwan's footfalls were silent as he and Dr. Wren navigated their way through the graveyard, following the precise instructions she had provided for the ritual. The weight of history bore down on them as they gathered the necessary components - the blood from his own veins, the earth from a long-forgotten grave, and the sacred hawthorn sprig.

"Are you sure this is the right place?" Safwan asked, his voice barely audible above the rustling leaves. He couldn't shake the feeling that they were being watched, as though the very air was alive with unseen eyes.

Dr. Wren nodded, consulting her worn leather-bound journal. "According to my research, this churchyard has been a site of power for centuries. It should serve as the perfect conduit for our purposes."

With painstaking care, they laid out the components within a circle of salt, carefully positioning them according to the ancient diagram etched into Dr. Wren's journal. Each item held its own symbolic significance, their energies intertwining to form a nexus of power that would fuel the incantation.

"Remember," Dr. Wren cautioned as they prepared to begin, "the words must be spoken with absolute conviction. You must believe in their power, or the spell will not take hold."

Safwan took a deep breath, steadying himself. In his mind's eye, he saw Aurya's haunted face, felt the anguish of their shared curse gnawing at the edges of his soul. He knew what was at stake, and he would not falter. He began to recite the incantation, each syllable heavy with desperation, determination, and hope.

As the ancient words filled the air, a shiver ran down Safwan's spine. The atmosphere around them grew heavy, crackling with an otherworldly energy that seemed to seep into his very bones. He could feel the power of the incantation taking hold, as though the spirits of the past had been awakened by his plea.

"Can you feel it?" he whispered to Dr. Wren, his heart pounding in his chest. "The energy... it's unlike anything I've ever experienced."

"Stay focused, Safwan," she urged him, her own eyes wide with awe and anticipation. "We must not lose control of the spell."

With renewed resolve, Safwan continued the incantation, his voice growing stronger, more resolute. If there was even a chance that this ritual could free him and Aurya from their eternal torment, then he would see it through - whatever the cost.

The candlelight flickered, casting eerie shadows on the walls of the dimly lit room. Safwan's voice wavered as he continued to recite the incantation, beads of sweat forming on his brow. The air around them seemed to grow still, the energy that had previously crackled within the room seemingly dissipating.

"Something's wrong," Safwan muttered through gritted teeth, panic rising in his chest. The scholar, Dr. Wren, furrowed her brow, her eyes scanning the ancient text before her.

"Perhaps you mispronounced a word or phrase?" she suggested, her voice laced with concern.

Safwan shook his head, determination reigniting within him. "No, I must continue. Aurya and I have suffered for too long – I cannot give up now." He took a deep breath, steadying himself, and began the incantation anew, each syllable ringing out with newfound fervor.

Dr. Wren watched Safwan intently, her fingers gripping the parchment tightly. "I believe in you, Safwan. You can do this."

As the words echoed through the chamber, Safwan felt an unfamiliar sensation begin to course through his body. It began as a ripple, a subtle shift in the very essence of his being. Gasping, he clutched at his chest, his eyes widening in realization.

"Dr. Wren," he whispered, his voice trembling, "it's working. I can feel it."

"Describe it to me," she urged, her curiosity piqued, even as she maintained her focus on guiding Safwan through the ritual.

"It feels... like the chains that have bound my soul for centuries are slowly loosening," Safwan explained, wonder and apprehension mingling in his voice. "My immortality is slipping away, replaced by something I haven't experienced in so long – mortality."

"Stay focused, Safwan," Dr. Wren reminded him gently, her eyes never leaving the parchment. "We must see this through to the end."

As Safwan continued the incantation, his heart pounded with a mix of fear and exhilaration. The sensation within him grew stronger, more insistent, yet he refused to let it distract him from the task at hand. He would do whatever it took to break the curse that had ensnared both him and Aurya, even if it meant facing the unknown consequences of the ritual.

"Whatever happens," he thought, "I must not waver. For Aurya's sake, and my own."

As the final words of the incantation left Safwan's lips, a heavy silence filled the room. The air itself seemed to hold its breath, as if waiting for some unseen force to make itself known. Safwan's body tensed with anticipation, but it was his face that bore the first signs of change.

"Dr. Wren," he murmured, his voice barely audible amid the stillness. "It's happening."

"Describe it, Safwan," she instructed, her gaze flicking from the ancient parchment to his rapidly transforming visage.

"Lines are forming on my face, creasing my skin as though time itself is catching up to me," Safwan said, a note of awe in his voice. He hesitantly reached up, tracing the newly-formed wrinkles with trembling fingers. "My eyes... they're losing their luster, fading like the embers of a dying fire."

"Stay strong, Safwan," Dr. Wren urged, her brow furrowed with concern. "You knew this would be part of the process. Remember why you're doing this."

He nodded, swallowing hard. "For Aurya. And for myself, to finally be free of this curse."

As Safwan aged before her very eyes, Dr. Wren couldn't help but marvel at the sheer power of the magic they had dared to unleash. She only hoped that the price they were paying would not prove too great. "We're almost there, Safwan. Just a little longer."

"Will it hurt?" Safwan asked, his voice cracking with vulnerability. "The end, I mean."

"None can say for certain," Dr. Wren admitted softly. "But you will finally have your peace, and Aurya will have her chance at life anew."

"Then let it come," Safwan whispered, steeling himself for whatever lay before him.

Miles away, Aurya sat in the dimly-lit solitude of her room, her thoughts consumed by the man who had given her both immortality and the chance to regain her humanity. She clutched at her chest as a sudden, overwhelming pain seized her, stealing her breath away.

"Something's wrong," she gasped, her eyes widening in terror. "Safwan... he's..."

As the pain intensified, Aurya knew without question that Safwan was dying – and with him, their shared curse. Though tears filled her eyes, she couldn't help but feel an aching gratitude for his sacrifice, intermingled with the crushing weight of loss.

"Goodbye, my love," she whispered into the darkness, even as her own heart began to beat with newfound life.

Chapter 11

اغفر لي "Forgive Me"

Moonlight spilled into the lavish bedroom, casting a silvery glow on Aurya as she stared blankly at the oil painting of an ancient forest that adorned one wall. She had taken refuge in Richie Davenport's secluded mansion, her heart a desolate wasteland since Safwan's death.

"Ah, there you are," came a voice from the doorway. Richie leaned against the frame, his eyes fixed on Aurya with unhidden curiosity. "You've been hiding away up here for days."

Aurya didn't respond, her gaze still locked on the painting. It was as if she could feel the chill of the forest scene, the icy tendrils of grief wrapping around her heart.

"I've been thinking about our conversation," Richie continued, stepping into the room. The floorboards creaked beneath him, but Aurya remained motionless. "About immortality and all that it entails." He paused, watching her closely. "I want to help you, Aurya. I want... to be your blood source."

At his words, Aurya finally looked at him, her eyes narrowing. She studied his face, seeking any sign of insincerity. Richie held her gaze steadily, his expression earnest.

"Richie, what do you expect in return?" she asked softly, her voice barely audible.

"Nothing," he replied without hesitation. "I'm not asking for anything but the chance to experience something beyond the mundane life I've been living."

"Immortality isn't a gift," Aurya warned, her tone heavy with the weight of centuries. "It's a curse, one that never ceases to take away those I care for." Her eyes glistened with unshed tears as she remembered Safwan's final moments.

"Maybe so," Richie conceded, inching closer. "But I can't help but feel drawn to it. Drawn to you, Aurya." He hesitated before adding, "I believe I can help ease your loneliness, even if just for a short while."

"Loneliness?" Aurya repeated, her voice cracking. "You don't understand what it's like to lose someone you... you loved."

"Perhaps not," Richie admitted, his eyes full of empathy. "But I do know what it's like to crave something more than this empty existence. To yearn for a connection that transcends the ordinary."

Aurya stared at him, her heart caught between hope and fear. Could she allow herself to trust him? To let him into her world of darkness and sorrow?

"Let me help you, Aurya," Richie urged gently, reaching out to place a hand on her shoulder. "Let me be a part of your life, no matter how fleeting it may be."

In that moment, Aurya saw a sincere desire in Richie's eyes — a hunger for something beyond the superficiality of his celebrity life. And perhaps, just maybe, she could find some solace in his presence.

"Very well," she whispered, her decision made. "But remember, Richie... this is a path from which there is no turning back."

The flames of the fireplace danced before Aurya's eyes, casting shadows on the walls of the dimly lit room. Richie's offer echoed in her mind — a chance for companionship, however fleeting. The weight of her grief threatened to crush her, yet she hesitated, fearing that she would harm him as she had harmed Safwan.

"Richie," Aurya began, her voice trembling. "There are things you must know about me... dark things."

"Tell me," he urged, his eyes never leaving hers.

She let out a shaky breath and looked deep into his eyes, searching for any signs of doubt or fear. Finding none, she continued, "I'm not like other people, Richie. I am... immortal."

"Immortal?" He leaned closer, curiosity igniting in his gaze. "You mean... like a vampire?"

Aurya nodded solemnly, steeling herself against the possible rejection. But instead, Richie's eyes seemed to widen with fascination.

"Then... you need blood to survive?" he asked, his voice barely above a whisper.

"Yes," she admitted, looking away. "It's a curse, Richie. And I am terrified of hurting you. But more than that, I'm afraid of what this curse might do to you if I accept your offer."

Richie's hand found hers, giving it a gentle squeeze. "Aurya, I understand the risks. But I can't shake this feeling that there's something powerful between us. Something worth exploring."

Aurya searched Richie's face, finding nothing but sincerity. She knew the dangers of allowing someone so close to her; she could not bear the pain of losing another loved one. And yet, the thought of having someone to share her eternity with, someone who understood and accepted her true nature, was intoxicating.

"Alright," she whispered, her resolve firming. "But remember, Richie... this decision will change your life forever. Are you certain you're prepared for the consequences?"

"More than anything," he assured her, his eyes filled with determination.

As Aurya gazed into the fire, she allowed herself to entertain the possibility of a connection with Richie – one that could ease her suffering and bring newfound solace to her immortal existence. And perhaps, just maybe, in each other's company, they could find the intimacy they both craved.

The full moon cast an ethereal glow on the sprawling grounds of Richie Davenport's secluded mansion, its silver light illuminating the darkness that had enveloped Aurya since Safwan's death. Her heart ached with every beat, as if it were longing to escape the confines of her immortal body.

"Are you sure about this?" Aurya asked, her voice strained by the weight of her emotions and the gnawing thirst within her.

"Absolutely," Richie replied, his eyes locked on hers with unwavering intensity. "You've shown me a world beyond anything I could have imagined. It's time for me to fully embrace it."

Aurya hesitated for a moment, considering the gravity of the choice before them. But Richie was already rolling up his sleeve, exposing the pale skin of his forearm. She could see the veins just beneath the surface, pulsing with life – with sustenance. Her fangs lengthened instinctively, ready to puncture and draw forth the crimson nectar she craved.

"Alright, then," Aurya murmured, her hand trembling as she reached for Richie's arm. "Just... please remember that I never wanted to hurt you."

"Neither did I," he whispered, his breath warm against her cheek. "But sometimes pain is necessary for growth, isn't it?"

As Aurya's fangs pierced the tender flesh of Richie's arm, she felt the familiar rush of ecstasy and agony intertwining. The rich warmth of his blood filled her mouth, quenching her parched soul. She drank deeply, each swallow forging an unbreakable bond between them.

Richie gritted his teeth as waves of pain and pleasure coursed through him. He marveled at the raw power he felt surging inside him, knowing that this sensation was nothing compared to what awaited him in the realm of immortality.

Aurya could sense Richie's thoughts, his excitement and wonder at the possibilities that lay ahead – a life unburdened by the mundane aspects of his celebrity existence. As she continued to drink from him, she felt her own heart begin to mend, the gaping void left by Safwan's absence slowly filling with the connection she now shared with Richie.

Time seemed to stand still as they remained in this intimate embrace, their souls entwined by the crimson thread of their newfound bond. And for the first time since Safwan's death, Aurya allowed herself to hope for something more than just eternal solitude.

"Thank you," she whispered, finally releasing Richie's arm and meeting his eyes with a mixture of gratitude and vulnerability. "I never thought I would find someone who could truly understand me... until now."

"Neither did I," he replied, pressing his fingers tenderly against the puncture wounds on his arm. "But here we are, Aurya. Together."

Aurya's eyes roamed over the vast library, its walls lined with ancient tomes, as Richie sat across from her, nursing his arm with an ice pack. Their bond now tethered them together, allowing them glimpses into each other's thoughts and emotions. They found solace in their shared silence, basking in the newfound understanding between them.

"Have you always been drawn to books?" Richie asked, breaking the quiet with a gentle inquiry.

"Ever since I can remember," Aurya replied, her fingers tracing the spine of a leather-bound volume. "They offer an escape, a chance to live countless lives beyond my own."

"Is there one that stands out among the rest? One that has truly touched your soul?" he persisted, his curiosity piqued.

"Strange as it may sound, it was a collection of human poetry. The words resonated with me, echoing the yearning for connection and belonging that I've felt for centuries," she confessed, warmth creeping into her voice.

"Could you recite one for me, please?" Richie requested softly, his eyes full of genuine interest.

With a hesitant nod, Aurya closed her eyes and began to recite the lines from memory, her voice weaving a tapestry of emotion that seemed to envelop them both. As she spoke, Richie listened intently, marveling at the raw vulnerability she displayed. He could feel the resonance of her immortal heart within the words, and it only served to deepen their connection.

"Thank you, Aurya," Richie murmured once she had finished. "I think I understand you a little better now."

"Likewise," she said, smiling faintly. "Your willingness to embrace this life - the darkness and the light, the pain and the pleasure - it's... refreshing."

"Perhaps we can find some balance in our existence, help each other navigate the complexities of immortality," Richie mused, his fingers intertwining with Aurya's.

"Perhaps," she agreed, allowing herself to entertain the possibility of a happier future. "Together."

As they spent more time together, Aurya's reclusive nature began to dissipate, replaced by a renewed sense of vitality. In Richie's presence, she found solace and understanding that had eluded her for centuries. And in turn, Richie reveled in the excitement and novelty that Aurya brought into his life - a far cry from the mundane aspects of his celebrity existence.

Their bond continued to strengthen, as they found themselves sharing not only their thoughts but also their dreams and fears, finding comfort in each other's company. It was a connection unlike any they had experienced before, and one they both knew they couldn't let slip away.

The moon cast a silver glow on the vast library, highlighting the leather-bound spines and golden lettering of the books that lined the walls. Aurya sat in a large armchair, her legs tucked beneath her as she lost herself in the pages of a 15th-century manuscript. She looked up when Richie entered, his eyes alight with excitement.

"Have you ever read anything like this?" he asked, brandishing a dusty volume in his hands. "It's an ancient grimoire that details rituals and spells to summon or banish otherworldly beings."

"Richie," Aurya replied, her voice tinged with amusement, "we have more than enough to deal with our own otherworldly nature without seeking out others."

Richie grinned, placing the book down on a nearby table. "I know, I know. But isn't it fascinating? Ever since we bonded, I can't get enough of the supernatural world. The thrill of the unknown, the danger – it's intoxicating."

Aurya studied him for a moment, noting the way his eyes sparkled with curiosity. She had to admit that his enthusiasm was infectious. As she closed her manuscript, she thought about how she had spent lifetimes safeguarding her heart from pain, but now she found herself drawn closer to Richie every day. His insatiable appetite for life breathed new life into her immortal existence.

"Alright," she conceded, rising from her chair. "Teach me something new, then."

"Really?" Richie's face lit up at the prospect. "There's a ritual here to communicate with spirits. We could try that."

"Very well," Aurya said, giving him a playful smile. "Show me what you've learned."

Over time, the secluded mansion became a playground for their shared passions. They explored the hidden passages and secret rooms, uncovering the secrets of the ancient house. They experimented with strange and exotic recipes in the kitchen, discovering new flavors to delight their immortal palates.

"Have you ever tasted anything like this before?" Richie asked as they sampled a dish infused with rare herbs and spices.

Aurya shook her head, savoring the complexity of the flavors. "I can't remember the last time I enjoyed food this much. You have quite the talent, Richie."

In the evenings, they curled up by the fireplace, sharing tender moments and deep conversations. As Aurya opened herself up to the possibility of happiness, she found that her once-reclusive demeanor began to fade, replaced by a newfound warmth and connection.

"Tell me about your life before all this," Aurya asked one night, tracing the contours of Richie's face with her fingertips.

"Before I met you, my life was a series of empty performances," he admitted. "I craved attention, but it never satisfied me. It felt hollow. Now I know what it means to truly live."

Together, they reveled in the pleasures that their immortal existence allowed – from exploring hidden worlds within ancient texts to creating art in the mansion's sunlit studio. And as they grew closer, Aurya realized that for the first time in centuries, she was not only surviving but thriving.

Aurya awoke to find herself entwined with Richie, their limbs tangled together like the roots of ancient trees. The morning light filtered through the curtains, bathing them in a gentle golden glow. She traced her fingers along the curve of his jaw, marveling at the softness of his skin. A surge of warmth filled her chest, and she allowed herself to bask in this newfound sense of belonging.

"Good morning," Richie whispered, his voice still thick with sleep. He opened his eyes, meeting Aurya's gaze with an affectionate smile. "Did you sleep well?"

"Better than I have in ages," Aurya admitted, feeling a profound gratitude for the comfort and solace that Richie brought into her life. Her grief over Safwan's death, once an overwhelming force, had begun to recede like the tides, leaving behind a sense of peace that she hadn't known was possible.

"Let's go for a walk in the gardens," Richie suggested, disentangling himself from Aurya's embrace. "I think we could both use some fresh air."

As they strolled amid the lush greenery and vibrant blooms, Aurya found herself drawn not only to the beauty of the landscape but also to the man beside her. Richie's wit and charm seemed to coax laughter from her like drops of water from a stone, and she reveled in the excitement and danger that came with their shared immortality.

"Have you ever considered traveling, Aurya?" Richie asked as they paused beneath an archway draped with ivy. "There are so many places in the world we could explore together."

"Before you, I only sought solitude," she confessed, her thoughts drifting briefly to the lonely years that had stretched out behind her. "But with you by my side, the world feels like a playground just waiting to be discovered."

"Then let's discover it," Richie said, his eyes alight with anticipation. "We can experience the wonders of the world together, and forge our own path through the centuries."

It was in that moment that Aurya realized how deeply her relationship with Richie had taken root. The solace she found in his presence had blossomed into something even more pro-found, a connection that bridged the chasm between their two souls.

"Richie," she murmured, reaching up to brush her lips against his, "I am truly grateful for the life we share, for the love that has grown between us. Together, we will dance through the ages, hand in hand, heart to heart."

As they embraced beneath the ivy-covered archway, Aurya felt the last remnants of her grief slip away, replaced by the warmth of Richie's love and the promise of countless adventures yet to come.

Moonlight streamed through the mansion's tall windows, casting ethereal shadows across the polished marble floor of the grand ballroom. Aurya and Richie stood at its heart, their eyes locked in a gaze that spoke volumes of their newfound intimacy.

"Tell me a story," Richie whispered, his breath warm against her ear. "A tale of love and longing from centuries past."

Aurya closed her eyes, her thoughts wandering through the mists of time as she recalled a tale that had captivated her once before. As her words painted vivid images of star-crossed lovers and ancient passions, an ache began to stir within her. It was the same longing she had felt for Safwan, the yearning for connection that had once consumed her.

"Have you ever lost yourself completely in another?" Richie asked, his voice tinged with vulnerability. "Felt as if your souls were intertwined, destined to be bound together for all eternity?"

"Once," Aurya admitted, her voice barely audible. "But now, I have found that connection again...with you, Richie."

"Then let us treasure this bond," Richie declared, his hand closing around hers. "Let us savor every moment, every shared experience, and make memories that will echo through the ages."

Aurya looked into his eyes, seeing reflected there the depth of their connection and the intensity of the path they would walk together. She could feel the last vestiges of her grief for Safwan ebbing away, replaced by a newfound sense of purpose and belonging.

"Richie," she whispered, her voice filled with wonder, "I never thought I could find solace in another's arms, but with you, I have discovered so much more than just comfort. In you, I have found my guiding star, a light to chase away the darkness that once shrouded my heart."

"Then let us be each other's salvation," he murmured, pulling her close and pressing his lips to her forehead. "Together, we shall navigate the complexities of this immortal life, and find joy in the simplest of moments."

As they danced beneath the silvery moonlight, Aurya felt a warmth spread through her body, a sense of peace that had once seemed unattainable. She realized she had found what she had sought in Safwan – a true connection, an intimacy that transcended time and distance.

"Thank you, Richie," she whispered against his chest, their hearts beating in perfect harmony. "Thank you for showing me that love can heal even the deepest wounds, and that together, we can forge a new path into the unknown."

And as they embraced, Aurya knew that their companionship would be the bedrock upon which they would build their future, providing them both with the solace and connection they had craved for so long.

Chapter 12

نسيان "Oblivion"

A single tear traced the curve of Aurya's cheek, catching the moonlight as it fell, a testament to the vulnerability she had not allowed herself in centuries. She stood before Safwan, her once-lover and eternal companion, whose eyes bore into her with an intensity that threatened to shatter the fragile resolve she had built.

"Is this truly what you desire?" Safwan asked, voice laced with disbelief and a hint of betrayal.

Aurya met his gaze, her dark eyes shimmering with unspoken emotions. "Safwan, please understand," she pleaded, her voice trembling. "I yearn for a life that includes aging, experiencing the joys and sorrows of mortality, and finding a sense of normalcy. I no longer wish to be shackled by immortality."

His jaw clenched, and the muscles in his neck tensed as he struggled to accept her choice. The air between them grew heavy with the weight of their intertwined histories and the unspoken pain of love and loss.

"Can you not see how this would make me happy?" Aurya continued, desperation evident in her tone. "My heart longs for something more than this endless existence, where everyone I love is but a fleeting memory."

Safwan closed his eyes briefly, attempting to reconcile his own desires for her happiness with the prospect of losing her to a mortal life. The eternity they had shared together stretched before him, filled with moments of passion, sorrow, and longing. He opened his eyes and saw the woman he had loved without reservation, now standing before him with an imploring look on her face.

"Your happiness has always been my priority," he admitted, the words leaving a bitter taste in his mouth. "But the thought of losing you forever, Aurya—that is a pain I cannot fathom."

"Would you rather see me suffer, trapped within this unending cycle?" she asked, her voice quiet but resolute. "I cannot continue like this, Safwan. I need to find my own path, one that allows me to experience the full spectrum of human emotion and connection."

As Aurya's plea unfurled before him, Safwan was forced to confront the depth of his love for her. His heart ached with the knowledge that it may never be enough to overcome the chasm that had formed between them. The thought of losing her to a mortal life, of watching her age and perish as he remained unchanged, tore at him like the sharpest of blades.

"Promise me," he whispered, his voice barely audible above the sound of their ragged breaths, "that when your time comes, you will not regret this decision."

Aurya hesitated, her eyes searching his face for any hint of doubt. In that moment, she realized that even if she could not guarantee a life without regrets, she needed to embrace the unknown in order to find solace and peace. With a determined nod, she replied, "I promise."

As they stood there, locked in a silent embrace, the weight of their immortal bond pressed down upon them, a reminder that though their paths may diverge, their love would remain a constant force throughout the ages.

The sun dipped toward the horizon, casting long shadows across Richie's opulent Calabasas garden. Aurya's heart fluttered like the delicate wings of a trapped butterfly as she watched Safwan's expression soften, his eyes betraying a deep sadness that mirrored her own.

"Very well," he murmured, his voice hoarse with emotion. "I cannot deny you the life you seek, Aurya. I love you too much to stand in your way."

Her relief was palpable, a sigh escaping her lips as she wrapped her arms around him, their immortal bodies entwined for what might be the last time. But even as they held each other close, the seeds of doubt began to take root in the fertile soil of Aurya's mind. Was Safwan truly willing to let her go, or would his love for her ultimately prove too powerful to overcome?

Suddenly, the garden gate creaked open, and Richie appeared, his handsome face lit by the warm glow of the setting sun. He approached them hesitantly, sensing the tension that hung heavy in the air like a cloak of melancholy.

"Is everything all right?" he asked, concern etched on his chiseled features.

"Richie," Aurya said, extricating herself from Safwan's embrace. "Safwan has agreed to let me live my life as a mortal, with you."

But as she spoke, a flicker of something dark and dangerous flashed across Safwan's eyes, a storm brewing on the horizon of his soul. The weight of centuries of love, jealousy, and power struggles threatened to engulf him, and he struggled to maintain control over the raging tempest of his emotions.

"Is that so?" Richie ventured, his tone cautious as he extended a hand toward Safwan. "I hope we can still be friends, despite everything."

As Safwan's gaze traveled from Richie's outstretched hand to his earnest face, the dam holding back his rage finally crumbled.

With a snarl of pure fury, he seized Richie's arm and twisted it violently, snapping the bone with a sickening crack. Richie cried out in pain, his body crumpling to the ground as Aurya looked on in horror.

"NO!" she screamed, her voice echoing through the garden like a banshee's wail. But even as the anguished cry tore from her throat, Safwan's actions continued unabated. He loomed over Richie's prone form, his fingers curling into claws as he prepared to strike the final, fatal blow.

"Please, Safwan," Aurya pleaded, tears streaming down her face as she desperately tried to come between him and his prey. "Don't do this. I beg you."

But Safwan's eyes were cold and unyielding, his love for Aurya drowned beneath the waves of jealousy that threatened to consume him. With a final, gut-wrenching scream, he plunged his clawed hand into Richie's chest, ripping out his still-beating heart as Aurya watched in abject terror.

"Forgive me, Aurya," he whispered, his voice barely audible above the sound of her ragged sobs. "But I cannot bear the thought of losing you to another."

As the sun dipped below the horizon, bathing the world in darkness, Aurya's life shattered into a thousand irreparable pieces, leaving her heartbroken and adrift in a sea of grief and despair.

The moon cast a ghostly glow upon the garden, its silvery light casting eerie shadows on the blood-soaked ground. Aurya's breath came in ragged gasps as she stared at the lifeless body of Richie, her heart shattering under the weight of her grief.

"Wh-why?" she whispered, her voice trembling with shock and betrayal. "Safwan, how could you?"

"Forgive me," he replied coldly, his eyes hard as stone. "But I would rather see you dead than in the arms of another."

Aurya's eyes widened in horror as Safwan brandished a wickedly curved knife, its blade glinting maliciously in the moonlight. Despite the pain that threatened to overwhelm her, she stood tall, refusing to cower before him.

"Then do it," she said quietly, her words laced with a sorrowful acceptance. "End my misery, if that is what you truly desire."

For a brief moment, Safwan hesitated, his love for Aurya warring with his jealousy and rage. But in the end, the darkness within him won out. With a guttural cry, he lunged forward, plunging the knife deep into Aurya's chest.

As the blade pierced her heart, Aurya felt a searing pain unlike anything she had ever experienced before. Her vision blurred, her body growing weaker with each agonizing second. And then, just as suddenly as it had begun, the pain vanished, replaced by an overwhelming numbness that spread throughout her entire being.

"Goodbye, Safwan," she breathed, her voice barely audible as she crumpled to the ground, her lifeless eyes staring up at the star-filled sky.

Safwan stared down at Aurya's body, his heart heavy with grief and remorse. He had acted out of anger, out of jealousy, and now the person he loved more than anything in this world was gone.

"Forgive me," he choked, his voice thick with tears. "I never meant for it to end like this."

But Aurya could no longer hear him. Her soul had departed, leaving Safwan alone with his guilt and despair.

The first light of dawn crept over the horizon, bathing the garden in a soft, golden glow. With trembling hands, Safwan gathered wood and kindling, preparing a funeral pyre for Aurya's broken body. He had taken her life, and now he would carry out the final act of love and respect by releasing her spirit from its immortal prison.

As the flames leapt into the sky, their fiery tongues licking at the heavens, Safwan knelt before the pyre, his eyes fixed on Aurya's face. Even in death, she retained a haunting beauty that seemed to defy the ravages of time.

"I am so sorry, my love," he whispered, his tears falling like rain upon the earth below. "May you find peace in the next life, free from the burdens of this one."

And as the smoke curled upward, mingling with the clouds above, Safwan allowed himself to be consumed by his grief, the weight of his actions pressing heavily upon his weary heart. For though he had claimed Aurya's life, he had also lost something far greater – the chance for redemption, for forgiveness, and for the love that had once burned so brightly between them.

Safwan held the urn containing Aurya's ashes close to his chest as he traversed the rocky cliffs of Portugal, the waves crashing relentlessly against the shoreline below. The wind whispered through the trees, carrying with it the scent of salt and nostalgia. As he approached the ancient fig tree that had once served as their secret meeting place, a flood of memories washed over him – passionate embraces, heated arguments, and stolen moments of fragile happiness.

He knelt beneath the gnarled branches, feeling the weight of the centuries bearing down upon him. This hallowed ground had witnessed the birth and death of countless lovers, yet it remained unchanged, a silent testament to the enduring power of love. Here, they had laughed and wept, locked in an endless dance of desire and despair.

"Forgive me, Aurya," Safwan murmured, his voice barely audible above the sound of the wind. He dug a small hole in the earth, mixing her ashes with the rich soil, entrusting her to the timeless embrace of the tree. "May you find peace here, beneath these roots that have borne witness to our love."

As he buried the last of her remains, the sun dipped below the horizon, casting long shadows across the landscape and darkening his grief-stricken heart. He unsheathed the knife that had stolen Aurya's life, its blade glinting menacingly in the fading light.

"Here, I shall join you, my love," he whispered, tracing the cold steel across his wrist. "In death, we shall be reunited, and perhaps find the redemption we so desperately sought in life."

Blood welled from the wound, staining the earth crimson as the first stars appeared in the twilight sky. As his vision blurred and darkness closed in, Safwan's thoughts turned to Aurya, her haunting beauty forever etched in his memory. His breaths grew shallower, each one a fragile thread unraveling the tapestry of his immortal existence.

"Forgive me," he whispered once more, reaching for her hand in the cold embrace of eternity. And as the lifeblood seeped from his veins, mingling with the soil that cradled Aurya's ashes, a final thought flickered through Safwan's fading consciousness: perhaps, in death, they would find the peace and redemption that had eluded them in life. For beneath the ancient fig tree, their love had blossomed and withered like the leaves that danced on the wind, bound by the threads of fate and the cruel passage of time.

Beneath the boughs of the ancient fig tree, the final whispers of Safwan's breath were carried away on a gentle breeze, mingling with the lingering scent of Aurya's ashes. The sun dipped low in the sky, casting long shadows that reached out like grasping fingers, as if to claim the souls of the tragic lovers for eternity.

"Was it all for naught?" a mournful voice echoed through the grove, its source unseen yet undeniably present. "Were their sacrifices in vain, their love doomed from the start?"

The wind stirred the branches above, as if in silent agreement, and the leaves rustled like the soft sighs of lost souls, seeking solace in the twilight of existence. A single tear, glistening like a drop of morning dew, traced its way down the cheek of an invisible observer, bearing witness to the untimely end of a love story that spanned centuries, continents, and countless lives.

"Perhaps," the anguished voice continued, "their love was too powerful, too consuming to be contained within the fragile vessel of mortality. It burned like the sun, searing all those who dared draw near and leaving naught but ashes in its wake."

A somber quiet settled over the scene, punctuated only by the steady thud of footsteps upon the earth as the unseen specter contemplated the fate of Aurya and Safwan. Their tragic tale, a testament to the strength and folly of the human heart, weighed heavily upon the spirit, inciting both sorrow and a deep sense of longing—a yearning for something greater, more transcendent than the confines of earthly existence.

"Yet, even in death, their love endures," the voice whispered, a quiet note of defiance amidst the despair. "For though they are gone, their story remains—an eternal reminder of the power of love, and the indomitable spirit of those who dare to dream."

As the sun dipped below the horizon, casting the grove in a cloak of twilight shadows, the wind carried away the last echoes of the lamenting voice. Yet within the silence that followed, a single word seemed to linger on the breeze—a word filled with hope, and the promise of redemption.

"Immortal."

www.ingramcontent.com/pod-product-compliance
Lightning Source LLC
Chambersburg PA
CBHW021001160726
47994CB00006B/2333